EASTBOUND, I THINK

Dear Dolly,

Pack lightly - but with
an open mind.
Continue to study your
Italian. Brava!

MARINA CALL

Marina Call

2 - DEC. - 2018

Disclaimer:

All characters are fictitious and any resemblance to actual persons,
either living or dead and purely coincidental and unintended.

Descriptions of architecture and cities are to the best of the
author's knowledge.

Author's Note:

There are several instances of four letter words in several languages
but are limited and not gratuitous.

Imagination and intellect cannot be contained.
There is no box.
M.C.

I

It was early in the day, or late for those returning home from a bacchanal evening. Oscar searched with slender fingers into the darkness of the black bag and felt the thick envelope as he waited for the signal. The conductor blew the whistle and the train doors unlocked. Walking towards the last wagon, he hoped it would be less crowded so he could stretch his long legs. The wheels pushed away from the Lisbon station and his body relaxed as the fields swished by with sunflowers tickled by black birds flying north. The train gained momentum and the compartment shook steadily with a constant rhythm.

He went back to the bag and felt the envelope still thick. It felt good between his fingers. He felt responsible and older. He was so appreciative to his uncle Nuno for this inheritance, which could not have come at a better time, allowing him to travel, his ever dream. Behind the envelope he found yesterday's *Expresso*, snatched from the kitchen table. He didn't think that anybody would be missing it. The numbers on the newspaper read *8 da agosto*, 1998. When he visualized the numbers in his head he saw 8 − 8 − 98. It was neat and related and he liked that. Then he thought of today's date and could not resist a smile thinking of   9 − 8 − 98. Order and sequence at its finest.

The projected four-hour trip would end in Badajoz, the capital of the region of Extremadura, located in southwest Spain, hugging Portugal, historically poor but culturally rich. After two days there he planned to visit Merida, most famous for its excellently preserved Roman theatre. After Merida he was unsure.

The train slowed down as soon as he saw the sign welcoming him to España. There it was—brightish blue with yellow stars around it.   And that was it; he was outside of Portugal, for the first time.   It was so anticlimactic, that he looked around to see if people were also feeling the disappointment, but the woman with the two small children was cleaning up spilled juice from the floor as her voice escalated and the man by him was reading the newspaper. The loudspeaker announced their entry into Spain in both Spanish and Portuguese.

The hot air dried his face as he stood on the top landing of the exit door and he shielded his black squinting eyes with sunglasses. He stepped off the train and walked until he found the Information Office. The man behind the glass started speaking to him in English. This was common as he was frequently mistaken for a foreigner in his own land. His British looks came with mixed reviews from the girls in his university; those who appreciated his unPortuguese looks admired his smooth, cream-colored skin that made his eyes and hair appear blacker than a widow's headscarf. Unfortunately, he had tended to be attracted to the women who yearned for the national beauty.

Oscar asked for a map and a list of museums in his best Spanish. *"Portugues,"* said the kind-faced man, who was balding and not bothered by it. He handed Oscar a map and mentioned a good little tapas bar where they served the "best *jamón* in the region." Oscar laughed softly when he remembered the guidebook had forewarned him that Spaniards were relentless for insisting that their version of the Portuguese cured ham, *presunto*, was better.

His intentions had been to see the Archeological Museum, but Paco, the bald man, had insisted that it was not very good and to view the MEIAC museum instead, which showcased modern and contemporary art. He followed the map and found the museum easily enough. Not an expert on this type of art, he found his mind wandering as he stared at a black canvas with a white dot in the upper right-hand corner. As soon as he could find the *Salida* sign he headed towards the tapas bar that Paco had recommended.

There was no sign in front of the bar that looked close to the circle on the map, so he walked in and asked if this was the Estrella Bar. A man with a thick mustache laughed and said it was down the road. He couldn't understand what was so funny about his question. Yes, his Spanish wasn't perfect but then again, their Portuguese wasn't either.

Why were the Portuguese expected to know Spanish, when the Spaniards never knew his language? Sure, they would try their *obrigado* and a few other words but hardly made a big attempt. He followed the directions and saw some children with white shirts and dark blue pants playing *futbol* in front of the cafe. There were a few empty tables outside, and Oscar became indecisive whether to sit inside or outside and risk the ball landing in his food. He stood there for a moment and eventually stepped in and asked if this was the Estrella Bar. *"Pues claro hombre, somos nosotros,"* the crooked-teeth bartender said. His black hair was shiny either from overused hair products or rubbing his hair after touching the olives' oil.

"Portugues, cómo te llamas?"

"Oscar," he replied. Trying to hide his nationality was not an option since these Spaniards must have been very used to their neighbors' accent. *"Muy bien Oscar, que te traigo?"*

Oscar peered through the glass countertop and saw that there were many choices. He pointed towards the large green olives and tuna mixed with red peppers. He almost forgot about the jamón! He asked for an extra large portion, *"Jamón, muy grande, por favor."*

"Adentro o afuera?" the waiter asked. It was now time to make a decision to his eating location. He decided that fresh air would be better after his train trip and pointed outside. His choices would be to either watch the *futbol*

game on the overvolumized television inside or watch some amateurs outside, so he thought he would be a little kinder to the children and not think bad of them.

Starving at this point, he looked at everything and wanted to shove it all in his mouth, but he knew there had to be an order to this. So he started with the olives and then went for the *jamón*. He figured the tuna would be last since it was the most overpowering in taste. After a couple of bites of the *jamón* he felt quite disappointed. Why was this known as the best *jamón*? Was the man at the train station possibly related to the owner, perhaps it was his brother or second cousin? This *jamón* was certainly good, but the best? That seemed like a strong word. He chewed a little more and took a generous drink of the Rioja wine. After the second glass he ate some of the crusty *pan* and delved into the *jamón* one more time. This time something changed: in his mouth was a delicious sensation of cured meat, as it ought to be, not too salty, with a nutty after taste at first then a second after taste in his mouth of something sweet. Not sweet like honey, but like a sweet salty kiss, when the taste rests on your lips long after the other has left.

So overtaken by this experience he realized he had closed his eyes to get the full impression of the flavor. With his insides full of *jamón* and olives, he reached for more bread and proceeded to the tuna dish. It was quite pleasant, but nothing like the *jamón*. He wished to keep the flavor in his mouth, but the tuna was so overpowering, he felt like he had cheated on his true love. More red wine helped mellow the tuna but it could not hide such an overpowering taste. He imagined a big tuna in the sea jumping out to fight with a pig. To the war, they would say, let us see who is the tastiest of this kingdom. He found himself laughing at this foolish thought!

The uniformed children had now disappeared and the other tables around him started filling up. These Spaniards must eat their lunch later than the Portuguese, he thought.

The noise from the other table started blending in because with so much screaming he could not make out words. He ordered a coffee and the waiter recommended the pineapple ice cream. He was expecting a couple scoops in a glass but instead got half of a pineapple planted in front of him. Someone had cut the pineapple and scooped out the flesh and proceeded to make the pulp into ice cream, then put it back in there and froze it. He took a bite to find the taste creamy, smooth and delicious and followed it up with some sparkling water.

After lunch, the waiter offered him two bottles of colored liquor; one was a strange shade of yellow and the other reddish orange. First he picked up the reddish one and tried it. Swishing it through his mouth it tasted like cough medicine with herbs and a bitter aftertaste. He cringed his forehead, took another sip of the sparkling water and decided it would be better to try the other one, in case he was missing out on something special. The urine colored thicker liquid went into his shot glass with ease and Oscar paused to smell it before ingestion. This one also smelled of herbs but without the sticky sweet smell of the other. Taking another whiff, he could almost smell grass and cinnamon. Perhaps his taste buds were confused, but nonetheless, he drank it carefully and did not immediately detest the taste, actually, after a glass full he decided to pour another one. If they have left it here for me, he thought, it must be because they don't mind if I indulge a bit more.

The sun reflected on the water from the fountain and his whole body felt relaxed. Leaning back in his metal chair, he closed his eyes and let the sun bundle him in warmth as he dreamt of taking a little rest, a *siesta*, as the Spaniards called it.

He thought of a bed made of liquid, with his body lying on top of it, transported by the breeze, soft winds passing by and cooling his sleep. After a short snooze, he peeked at his clock and saw that it was almost 16:00.

Confirmed by the paper in his bag, he had two hours before he was allowed to check in to his hostel.

Oscar asked for the bill and sobered up when he stared at the paper that read 1000 pesetas. The currency he held in his pocket was from across the border and he came to the realization that since the museum had been free, he really had not paid for anything until now.

How could he have forgotten to exchange money? What a novice traveller he was! He flagged the *camarero* and showed him his Portuguese escudos. "Pesetas, hombre" replied the waiter and pointed him towards an Exchange sign down the street. Oscar left his identification card as assurance that he would return.

The transaction was not difficult: he passed Escudos through the glass window and they gave him Spanish pesetas. The Spanish bills had the face of the Spanish King, Juan Carlos II. He stared at the attractive face. He was sure that the portrait was much younger than the King's current age.

Oscar placed one of the bills in his secret wallet compartment. His mother, Odette, would enjoy this as a keepsake. She loved all the gossip about the Spanish monarchy and the British, of course, especially since Portugal's was now long gone.

He returned to the Cafe Estrella, paid his bill and thanked the waiter. He threw his bag across his shoulder and walked away with a feeling of accomplishment.

II

Oscar headed towards the Plaza de España and found a bench underneath an old tree and studied his map. Badajoz was a very difficult name to pronounce, he thought. Spaniards had their strong j's and z's that sounded like a lisp. He opened his Let's Go Spain! travel guide and read a little bit on the history of this city, but found no information on the meaning of its name. The city was quite busy with a lot of energy. More children in white shirts and blue pants and skirts passed by. This time they seemed a bit more organized and looked to be following a teacher. The women were also dressed in a lot of white with long black hair piled up high on their head or flowing over their tanned shoulders.

The Spaniards were very loud, much louder than the Portuguese. What startled him was how different the women looked; they were so attractive, much better looking than in Lisbon. With their round faces and expressive eyes, he thought he could fall in love ten times before reaching the river. He smiled at one of them, with the red shirt, but she looked away and whispered something in her friend's ear. The shorter friend with the black skirt and white blouse kicked her friend in the ankle and they both sheepishly smiled and laughed together. So many smiles going around this place, you would forget it was one of the poorest regions in Spain. That goes to say that if there is sun, there is at least hope. Imagine the poorest regions of Russia, with only snow and clouds to look forward to. There must be hope for something better—vodka perhaps.

Oscar was feeling a little giddy and relaxed from the red wine. He started smiling more than he was aware of and forgot about his canine teeth that stuck out a bit too much, making him look like a drunken vampire. His thin nose matched his thin body. He really did not look as Portuguese as he would have liked. His height was

11

advantageous, better views in a crowd, but his thin nose made him look suspicious. His dark eyes were set back, neither ugly nor impressive, just average, sparkling best when he smiled but then the teeth caught the attention. His favorite asset was his black shiny hair; it woke up with an undulating wave to the right making him look full of ideas.

He was living his dream of travelling outside of Portugal. When Elena had asked him where he was heading, Oscar replied, "Eastbound, I think." North was Galicia which did not interest him as much and no other choice was left as the ocean surrounded him to the west and south. Portugal was at such an interesting place in Europe, the western most point. His family had travelled extensively throughout Portugal, and his favorite place was the Madeira Islands. His mother Odette was the only one who had travelled out of the country, to England. She had gone there for her profession, which was a seamstress and although her favorite task was making men's suits, she mainly worked on wedding dresses and other elaborate ensembles for Lisbon's high society. She preferred the suits because they were more sensible in lines and could be adjusted more easily, so every time she took work home Oscar and his sister had to hear about what a nuisance the dress fabric was. Her voice was usually muffled as she drowned in tulle, chiffon and silk. Oscar and his sister did not really hear her comments, or were rather numb to them after so many years of complaints. Elena, ironically, showed no interest in her mother's profession. As for Oscar, he was quite adept, especially for a man. He washed his clothes weekly, bleaching the whites, separating the darks, starching the collars and pressing all cotton. He would always look both ways when he was ironing before working on his underwear. Afraid someone would think him strange, he felt they were more comfortable if they were ironed. His socks he would skip, but all else was put under the iron's warm caress.

As he was wondering whether or not the hostel had an iron, he passed by a Laundromat. He pressed his thin, pointed nose against the glass for a closer look. There were washing machines along the back wall, dryers on the right, and a large table in the center with two young boys splayed on their stomachs zooming toy cars around the table legs. Above, their mother folded little stacks of red shirts, yellow bathing suits and white underwear in tower shapes. She spread out a large blue and white towel with a crab in the center. Oscar's smiling eyes met hers and she hopelessly restrained a smile. She did not look older than 22, her face adorned with no makeup, golden skin glowing from the heat inside the laundry and the last 30 days of summer. Her long dark hair was held up by a tight ponytail on top of her head. Her green eyes looked directly at Oscar, and he left her gaze and the shaded canopy area with his heart aflutter.

The burning sun and thoughts of her face followed him for blocks. Were those her boys? They did not look as tanned as she did, but then again, he was not as tanned as his mother. Would that cause someone to think him not his mother's biological son? He had never really thought about that. His father joked that he was the milkman's son because he was *leitoso*. Elena looked just like her father, their hands and feet were identical. Eerie almost.

Why did he feel so different from his family? It felt like something was wrong with them, not him. They had no interest in leaving Portugal; he could not wrap his head around this. Well, his mom would have liked to, but she was not strong enough to impose her will.

The sun was beating down and after a long while of walking he stopped below a canopy to check his map. Was he still walking in the right direction? The map confirmed that he was still ok. He turned towards the big window and saw a red crab staring at him. It lay on a blue background. It was the same towel that the girl was folding at the Laundromat.

He went inside and breathed in the cool air. He explained to the shopkeeper that he wanted the towel in the front window, but she led him to the back of the store. *"Estos son MUCHO mejores,"* the woman said and kept shoving different towels in his hands and making him feel the cotton between his thumbs and index fingers. Yes, she was right, the cotton was thicker and softer but he was not interested in the better quality.

"Bon, bon" he said, then replacing it with *"Bien, Bien."*

"Ah, Portugues? *De Lisboa?"* she asked, feeling very sure that all Portuguese were from Lisbon.

"Si, Lisboa," Oscar said. She smiled, very proud of herself.

"Estos bon?" She asked, pointing to the other towels. *"No, gracias,"* he disagreed. He really wanted the towel with the red crab that reminded him of the green-eyed woman. *"Ésta,"* he pointed again to the crab towel. The shopkeeper nodded her head.

Oscar took out his pesetas and asked how much the towel would cost. *"Quinientas,"* she said and wrote it down to make sure he understood. While waiting for her to get his change he looked around the trinket counter. There were these bright colored lighters next to his right hand. He questioned himself as to whether he needed one; he did not even smoke. Well, in the end he decided to buy one as an appeasement to the shopkeeper. She smiled and folded the towel again, making sure all the creases were perfect, and put the yellow lighter on top. With the red plastic bag in hand, he exited and the sound of the little bell bid him farewell. Pure brightness found his eyes and he immediately covered them with his sunglasses.

III

The river had looked much closer on the map. He arrived sweating, and his ideas of a quick dip changed when he saw that the water was more brown than clear. There were no swimmers. There was no smell of coffee and candy rising from carts with red and white umbrellas. Worst of all, there were no women with skirts pulled up above their knees trying to get a tan with knotted shirts to tan their midriffs. There was no one really, just him. Well, almost only him. Small dots of blood on his arms revealed that it was the mosquito's witching hour, not a limb left for pardoning.

He felt foolish standing there with his bright red plastic bag. What a tourist he must appear like to others! Not willing to give up quite yet, he continued towards the big modern bridge. It had large wires connecting it from top to bottom, trying to mirror a sail of some sort. Unsure of its functional or aesthetic purpose, the design was quite fine but not what he was in the mood for. He had expected a nice riverfront with rowboats to rent, the chatter of the Spaniards on a sunny day, the smell of something sticky and sweet.

Instead he was alone and already missed the chatter in the cobblestone streets with the energy of the people walking by. While walking toward the bridge he questioned himself. Should he turn back or keep walking? He proceeded through the interior streets towards the bridge. This part of town was probably not recommended by the Tourist Office. No machine guns in sight, but poverty, yes. There were many gypsies in this area, and gypsies were very good at stealing. He held tighter to his red bag, feeling ridiculous.

Reprimanding himself for trying to walk off the beaten path, he continued at a brisk pace, lowering his shoulders to look relaxed and reminding himself not to look up at buildings as tourists do, always giving themselves away. He changed his face to appear determined and bored, giving the sense of a local.

These did not look like the buildings in the old historical portion of the town. Factories, or electrical plants—he did not want to stop to look too intently. He saw some faded signs, no longer lit up, and decided not to look up at them. His sunglasses would help. Why had he not thought about that? He searched inside his pocket but did not feel them, after practically patting himself down, he realized they were on top of his head. He put them on his eyes and felt ridiculous for his forgetfulness.

The sidewalks in this area were cracking out of the ground. There was dust in the air, on the walls, on the streets, on the cars, on the trucks, on the dogs, on the cats, on the street signs, on the trees and on the overhanging electrical wires. Oscar could feel even his throat full of dust and began coughing when a grumbling truck drove by. In that instant a loud obnoxious sound started down the street. When he looked up he found a dirty arm and hand nearing his face at full speed and swooshing down. He instantly turned away and the red bag lay ripped on the ground.

Oscar checked for his wallet but it was still in his pocket. His glasses! The thief had taken his glasses. He was incredulous. Upon realizing this, he waved his hand up in the air and started yelling profanities in Portuguese. The observers did not understand the specific words, but they understood his intentions.

After gathering himself, he started walking, now truly looking upset and definitely not looking like someone anybody would like to approach.

The large mirror of a truck reflected the scratches on his face. Oscar was disappointed with himself. How could he have been robbed by a dumb kid on an old motorcycle?

16

A true mirage appeared ahead. A 15-foot statue of Triton spit out water from its mouth into a large fountain. Thirst overcame him and he drowned his face until the water was running down his checkered button-up shirt.

Ding dong, ding dong! Loud bells rang the six o'clock hour. The moment had come to find his hostel. But first, a quick stop at the train station to get his backpack.

IV

Oscar reached the top of the stairs of the grand train station and felt proud that he had remembered where the lockers were located. His bag felt very heavy compared to the dumb plastic bag he had carried all day and blamed it for drawing attention from the thief. Well, he laughed to himself, this large backpack probably would too, but its brown and mustard yellow design was not as loud as red, which screams 'look at me, I am here."

Oscar enjoyed the busyness of the train station; the energy made him feel safe, part of a group, a bubble in the ocean moving with a purpose, some arriving, some departing, but always moving. It was in the stillness he found discomfort, a loneliness others yearned for, a solitary state that he abhorred. He circled around before leaving, going to the Timetable section to see what cities connected in and out of Badajoz.

"Fuuuuck! Bloody hell! *Que mierda!*" Oscar heard at close distance. He turned around to see a guy about his age, 25 or perhaps he was 30, he was not very good at guessing, but very similar in height, with dark hair like his own. They could have been cousins because of how similar they were in body type but then this guy took off his glasses and he realized that he was the uglier duckling of the two. His eyes were lighter than his, almost gray; his eyelashes were like unmowed grass in the spring, spiky and long. His sister Elena always commented on this tiny feature in our body's design. He would have never have noticed this, but Oscar respected his sister as the grand knower of all things women, so he listened when she spoke. His better half's lips were fuller than his own and his skin was more tanned. It was like looking at an idealized version of himself. He felt instantly mesmerized. This young man seemed upset.

"You ok man?" Oscar asked him.

"NO, *para nada*, no, I am not!" the other responded. "They have cancelled my train trip and I am never going to make it to my cousin's wedding in Granada."

"Why don't you rent a car?" Oscar asked, thinking he was helpful.

"*Gilipollas*, if I had the money to rent the car, I wouldn't be at the train station, right?" he responded, matter-of-fact, as though Oscar was an imbecile.

"*Bueno, hasta luego*," Oscar responded, incredulous as to the insanity of the people in this town, their blood boiling quicker than across the border.

Suddenly, he got a tap on the back and turned around to see his evil twin staring at him.

"Now what?" Oscar blurted at him.

"Sorry, I was rude. I am just really stressed out. I am Daniel," he said stretching out his hand.

Oscar stared at his hand and slowly shook it, feeling confused, for this sudden change of mood. "Oscar," he said clearly, but dryly.

Daniel became friendlier, asking Oscar for his advice on where to stay and what parts of the city he had seen. Oscar shared the little information that he knew, more about where not to go. They stood there talking for a while, and Oscar finally took off his heavy backpack.

Now it was Daniel telling him about the places to go— not that he had been, but had heard of. He was so sure of himself, that he could find this underground communist gathering point a friend of a friend's cousin had told him about. Oscar began to wonder why he was talking to this guy, but he had some interesting stories, so their conversation continued.

Oscar offered to help Daniel find a room in town, and they walked side-by-side looking for a vacancy. They were rejected three times. The hotel owners explained that there was a very important bullfight and a music concert on Saturday night. Paco, the bald guy at the train station, had failed to mention any of this, Oscar thought. They were inching closer to Oscar's hostel. He secretly hoped there would not be a spot for Daniel, mixed in with a wish that there would be. Daniel's moodiness was fascinating, like a boat inside a glass bottle, but Oscar did not feel that he could figure out this character very well and it made him uncomfortable.

They both waited for the key keeper to return and the news was that there was one single room left. *"Numero 7,"* she said and they followed the corridor to have Daniel leave his things.

V

After showers and clean shirts, the newfound "friends" were starving, and Oscar felt in control for the first time all day and led Daniel to his favorite restaurant, which was laughable since it was the only restaurant he knew.

The waiters announced, *"El portuges!"* when he showed up and it made Daniel eye him with esteem. They ordered the *jamón*, of course, and tried other tapas that the waiters recommended. The outside tables looked quite different in the dark and the futbol players were nowhere in sight and replaced with shadows from the candles. As the night went on the tables filled up more, with girls sitting on each other's laps or on the laps of a lucky man's, but not on Oscar's and not on Daniel's, even though the girls mainly looked at the latter, and less at the former.

What had started out as an awkward encounter proved to be a good match. The young men got on well, with rare moments of silence. Daniel told Oscar about his interesting roots. He was half Spanish and half British.

"I apologize for the embarrassing story. Well, it is not embarrassing so much as cliché. We are the typical Brits. Living in a country with shitty weather, and so my parents, when I was 10, decided to take a holiday down south. I guess they promised them *el oro y el moro*."

"What does that mean?" Oscar asked inquisitively.

Smiling, Daniel responded, *"El oro y el moro* means the gold and the Moor. Back during the time when the Moors ruled over Spain it was all about the gold and Moors, so it is another way to say they promised them everything."

He continued, "They showed my parents these plans of a development area they were building along the eastern coast, called Costa Blanca. The whole family got flown over there, and we got to see a bunch of empty land close by the sea. There were several duplex or *casas bajas*, how they call them here, and they seemed nice enough. My father has told me that the prices for those of us who made quid, were spectacular. So they signed up to buy one of these houses.

"It is strange that I remember it so well. Possibly could have been one of my happiest summers. We rented this apartment that overlooked the Mediterranean Sea and my three siblings and I just marched through the apartment singing this mock of a national anthem that our Spanish neighbors had taught us. It was about Franco, the late dictator and his white butt."

"What?!" Oscar said, laughing, "I can't imagine a stranger song than that."

Daniel started humming to himself. " I think I remember the tune... *Franco, franco tiene el culo blanco y su mujer tambien! Lo lavan con Ariel.*" Daniel explained that Ariel was pronounced A-ryél with just two syllables, not like the mermaid in the Disney movie. Ariel was a laundry detergent and the song went that Franco and his wife both had a white butt and that they washed it with Ariel.

They both started laughing. It was hard to tell if it were the song's lyrics, Daniel's out-of-tune voice or the wine, but Daniel kept singing motivated by Oscar's laughter. The table of Spaniards next to them had also drunk their share of wine and joined them in song.

The waiters looked at them and then at their watches, The two groups got to talking and invited Oscar and Daniel to a party they were going to after the bar. The boys looked at each other and shrugged their shoulders to agree, "Why not?"

"*Por qué no?*' Oscar said to them and shortly after they were all on their way.

22

This other group was made up of five people. They were all Spaniards, mainly from close to Badajoz, two from the north region of Galicia. Oscar noticed that their accent was somewhat easier to understand and he figured that because their region touched his Portugal, that they would be more akin to him.

The seven twisted their ways through the streets with blurry lights and undulating sidewalks. It was hard to tell where they were going since they would turn right then left; they could have been going in circles for all Oscar knew. He found himself at the back of the group and decided to move quicker and catch up. He spotted Daniel towards the front talking to the female brunette whose head barely reached his chest. She had long curly hair touching her rear. With the humidity of the night, her hair was sprayed in all directions, and when she swung her hair side to side it made it appear that Daniel had a horsetail with the shadows.

The bass of the music could be heard louder and louder as they neared the dismantled building. Oscar could sense he was back in the outskirts of the town, but the excess of wine prevented him from feeling apprehensive.

The walls were lit with candles on the floor that had so much wax overflowing that it was hard to walk around them without getting close to the flame. It seemed like an accident waiting to happen. As they descended the stairs the air became warmer and Oscar reveled in the wall art. The walls were a creamy earth color and were painted or graffitied with large figures with human bodies and rabbit heads. The mouths were large X's and at the top of the X were two eyes framed with upside down eyebrows.

Besides rabbit-humans, there were bird drawings of larger-than-life winged creatures with bird bodies and human legs holding them up. Dark red curtains framed a black painted window with a large white mouth and orange sinister eyes. Out of the mouth protruded Dracula teeth.

Oscar licked his own vampire teeth and exposed them at the painting with a loud roar. The group's laughs echoed from the expanse of the cathedral ceilings. They descended the three flights of stairs holding onto the old wood and metal railings in order not to trip on the broken pieces of marble steps. The steps were so smoothly worn down that the curly haired short girl fell on her fat bottom and more laughter bounced off the walls. More rabbits highlighted by black candles and framed with the thick red velvet curtains accompanied them as they reached closer to the dizzying music. Once the downward spiral ended, Oscar felt extremely thirsty and spotted a makeshift bar at the far right of the large room they had entered. The whole group must have had the same idea because their sweaty bodies led them towards the liquid bar.

The tall walls were adorned with a large Triton figure in the center. It was an abstract version of the fountain Oscar had seen earlier that day. But instead of other Roman gods, it was surrounded by black-skinned mermaids and evil-looking fish with wide open mouths exposing sharp teeth.

The drawings were mesmerizing, and Oscar could not keep his eyes off of them. He drank his bubbly soda swiftly, then asked for another. After so much wine, he decided he better slow down and hydrate his body. Daniel did not heed the same warning; he ordered several whiskey shots and then ended up with a rum and ginger ale cocktail.

The music was contagious. The Galicians were jumping up and down, the curly haired girl was swaying her hands above her head, and strands of her wild hair were wet and getting stuck on her fingers. Daniel was putting the moves on her at this point, touching her face, then her shoulders, down her back and to her ample butt. She started falling towards the floor and Daniel saved her before she hit the ground. Her dancing attempts were becoming more uncoordinated and her drink was decorating the floor underneath them.

Oscar was checking out her butt which was too big for her body; it looked like she had put padding inside of her pants but he knew no woman would do that, or would they? He didn't understand women very well, so he discarded the attempt of an answer. While thinking of her butt he thought of Franco and his white butt and his wife all prancing around with Daniel and his siblings as they marched around his apartment. He laughed out loud to himself and enjoyed his own moment while looking at all the big mouths with their open faces and teeth matching his own.

He could have looked like a mad man to an observer, standing there with good posture, leaning on the bar, laughing alone with his big open mouth. He did not mind and felt good in his white skin that evening. In awe his mouth remained, as his eyes pierced across the room.

Walking towards him was the girl from earlier that day. He spotted those green eyes through the music, sweat and moving bodies around him. Was she looking at him, or someone behind him? Could it really be her? Where were her two boys?

No longer with a glass window between them, Oscar stood even taller and wiped his longish hair from his eyes. Her long shapely legs glided towards him and he admired her beautiful body as she approached him. Two thin silver straps crossed her shoulders and her dress was moving with ruffles and lace in gold and bronze. If the Academy Award statue had a wife, she would have been its human equivalent. Her bronzed cheeks were glowing, and Oscar leaned forward to close the distance between them.

"*Hola,*" he greeted her, assuming that she was Spanish.

25

"*Hola, tu eres el chico de la Lavatienda?*" she asked.

"*Si, eres de aqui, de Baa...da ..joz?*" he struggled to pronounce the city's name and probably did a worse job than usual due to his nerves. Oscar was feeling thrilled she had recognized him, but silly that he had run away from the store earlier.

"I also speak English," she said.

"Oh good," he responded. This was a relief since his English was better than his Spanish.

"My name is Oscar, and you?" he said impatiently wanting to know her name.

"Monica," she said and leaned in to give him the customary two kisses on the cheek that Spaniards affectionately always gave.

Oscar wondered what his two-day old facial hair felt like on her golden skin. She had kissed him close, not in the air and her warm breath smelled of juniper.

"It's muy *caliente aqui*. You must be thirsty, can I get you something to drink?"

"*Claro,*" she said and ordered a gin with 7-up.

Oscar paid for it, and when he had put his money away she asked him, "Aren't you thirsty? Can I get you something to drink?"

"No, no thank you, I will order something later."

"Not fair," Monica said. "You got me a drink, so let me get you one."

"*Vale*," he responded, trying to say the Spanish words he knew well.

Her offer surprised him. He could not remember a woman ever offering to buy him a drink. Well, Elena would all the time when they would go out, but she was his sister and that didn't count.

Monica nodded her head towards the bar and indicated it was his turn to order. He leaned over and asked the bartender for a gin and 7-up. He had never tried this combination, but it sounded refreshing and that way he would not have to order a non-alcoholic drink and appear to be a prude, or on the other hand, have to think up another cocktail combination.

Monica seemed pleased with his choice, smiled at him and gave the bartender some pesetas that she took out from her golden purse. She was a glowing combination of all the shades of gold, silver and bronze he had ever seen.

"*Gracias*," Oscar said as he raised his glass and they cheered with plastic cups.

"Where are your little boys?" he asked, curious to know more about her.

"Oh, my nephews! Those are the terrible two! Diego y Manuel. They are my sister's twin boys, and I was watching them as she went to get her haircut. When we arrived at my sister's house that afternoon, Diego realized that he had forgotten his favorite car under the folding table, so I had to walk back with him to get it or else we were going to have to hear about it all night. I love them to pieces, but after two weeks living closely with them in my sister's apartment I am ready to take a break."

Oscar was relieved that she did not have children and a husband waiting at home for her.

"What are you doing here, on vacation from Portugal?" Monica asked.

His accent could not be hidden. "Yes, this is my first time out of Portugal and I've been wandering the city today. I am heading east after this."

He did not mean to say it so abruptly, to cut the possibility of another meeting or spell out the obvious information that he was moving away from the city where she lived.

"I will be heading out of here soon, but Southbound, or rather Southwest bound. Can you say that?" she asked.

"Sure! Where do you live?" he asked her this time louder than before since the music was turned up for this techno song.

"In Granada, it is five and a half hours south from here. I was living in London for a while but am back at home."

"Were you working or studying in London?" he asked.

"Well, a bit of both. I took some courses to improve my English and was working part-time teaching Spanish in a Catholic elementary school. This was my first flight out of Spain, so don't feel bad if you have never left Portugal."

"My mother took some courses in London before I was born." Oscar said, "She is a seamstress in Lisbon."

Monica seemed very interested in this line of work and he explained to her more about his mother's profession.

Suddenly, Daniel came up to them and introduced himself to Monica. Oscar stared at Monica to see if she seemed interested in Daniel. She appeared neutral. Daniel put on his charm and the curly-haired short girl did not appreciate it. Leaning on his chest, she tried to show that they were together and Daniel whispered to Oscar and Monica, "She is drunk. What do you say if we get out of here and step into the fresh air?"

Leaving the mythical animals behind them, they climbed the stairs to find the main entrance full of people waiting in line to get in. To Oscar it was incredulous that at this hour there would be a large line, but because of the festivities many more outsiders were in town.

Finally free of the sweaty crowds and cramped spaces, the group of seven walked towards the river. "*Tienes fuego?*" Monica asked as they walked with arms brushing. When Oscar's face looked confused, she gesticulated with her thumb, moving it up and down. Oscar reached inside his pocket and used his new yellow lighter. Monica's eyes illuminated her smile, and Oscar rested his lips swiftly upon her cheek. He tasted Juniper berries mixed with salt. But it was not possible, as they were far from the salty water. For him, all things good smelled like the ocean.

The full moon would have helped to light the night, but the followers went behind the leader who knew the city, and through the dusty paths they arrived to the banks of the river. Oscar could not tell if this was the part of the river where he had been before, so he started searching for the large bridge. He could not find it, looking to the right or to the left. The river bent in different directions and did not allow him to identify his location.

They stripped off their shoes and the sand felt smooth between their feet, after walking through prickly grass. Shirts, shorts, dresses, underwear, shoes were flying through the air. Cellphones were used as flashlights to indicate the way and Daniel was the first one to jump in. The rest of the group followed.

The water refreshed their bodies and made them feel awake. Oscar tried floating and Daniel shoved him down to the bottom with his strong arms. The bottom of the river was muddy and filled with more sharp grass. He even felt something cold and round. Diving down to get it, he figured out it was a glass bottle. Not sure what to do with it in his hand, he dove down again to place it carefully at the depth of the river floor. The sound of crickets accompanied them and the fireflies looked like fairies with their liquored eyes.

"*Tengo hambre!*" someone yelled. "*Yo también!*" another responded. Not long after everyone chimed in that they were also hungry, blurting suggestions of what would be delicious at the moment.

"*Churros con chocolate!* Pizza! *Un bocadillo!* Kebab! Chinese food! Watermelon!"

Shaking off their bodies in the black night, the clothing went back on each corresponding owner except for a pair of socks, and a small purse that was forgotten.

With purpose, the group followed the lights of the city and found a café. They arranged and rearranged themselves at the outside tables, knocking over salt shakers and throwing salt over their shoulders for good measure.

The treasures included piping hot chocolate with mounds of white swirls, cold Coca-Cola's sweating down their glass bottles, potato chip bags that crackled when opened and chewed, and a foot-long piece of crusty bread. Manchego cheese was cut in perfect triangles and arranged on a chipped blue and white plate. The second tray had even more cracks and held salami, sobreasada and *jamón*.

"You still want c*hurros?*" The waiter asked the group as they were stuffing their faces and talking between.

"*Sí hombre!* 4 *raciones!*" Daniel blurted out. The waiter was not sure if they would eat it all, but he sure hoped they had enough money to pay.

VI

Oscar woke up with the sunrays plucking his eyelids open. He bashfully opened his eyes and looked around his surroundings. He shut his eyes again because he could not place where he was and his head was pounding drums. Fifteen minutes later he took the pillow off of his head and opened up his eyes, staring at the many cracks in the ceiling. The trim work was poorly done and it looked as if an earthquake had passed through the room. Some poor painter must have tried to cover up the gaps with extra paint and a shiny sheen, but they were still apparent. The yellow of the room bounced off the sunlight to make it appear almost white. He realized that part of that pounding was not only in his head but also outside. Tap, tap, tap, pause, tap, pause, tap, tap, pause, tap, tap, tap, tap, pause. It almost sounded like some kind of secret code–like when one calls SOS. Unfamiliar with the significance of the pauses and taps, he waited for them to stop. Creaking doors and footsteps headed towards him and boom! He fell on the floor when his own door exploded with a thunder of knocking. Untangling himself from his sheets that twisted around him he got up and asked in an angry tone, "Who is it?"

A familiar voice responded, *"Yo, gilipollas*! It is Daniel, open up!"

"Imbecil," Oscar said to him while opening the door.

"Imbecil. Is that imbécil in Spanish? Cool."

"Why are you here so early? I am exhausted and want to sleep a couple more hours."

Daniel did not seem to be interested in Oscar's wants. "We are going to Granada today! Don't you remember?"

"Today?' Oscar looked confused. "I do not remember that! But then again, I don't remember walking home." He placed his fingers on his head and started rubbing his temples backwards, attempting to comfort his wine-filled brain.

"At first we had talked about waiting a few days, but the radio this morning said that they are no longer on strike today so we can get the train down to Granada."

"No! I want to see Merida and other sites before heading down south," Oscar said, feeling confident that would deter Daniel from insisting it had to be done today.

"*No te preocupes hombre!* It is not as if the Roman theater is going anywhere. The Merida girls are anxious for visitors, so they will be happy to see you whenever you arrive."

"No se. I am not sure, I have barely seen Badajoz either."

Oscar interrupted, "Yes you have, there is not much more to see."

"But what about the Alcazaba? I have only been to the modern museum and still need to see the Museo de Artes Finas, and travel to the other cities in Extremadura. Granada can be done at the end of the week."

Daniel responded, "*No seas gilipollas!*"

"*Imbecil,* stop insulting me! Why are we in such a rush?"

"Oscar, you are a train wreck. Don't you remember my long explanation last night about how I had spoken to my sister and she said there were going to be a bunch of festivities with my family this week. I am talking wicked food, drinks, etc. The strikes have ended early; it is a sign!

I have already packed my stuff, we can get our second breakfast of the day and there is a train leaving at 10:45am. I will help you pack."

Oscar was still standing barefoot in his boxer shorts as Daniel was full dressed in shorts and a collared La Coste shirt and brown leather sandals. Daniel was holding his backpack in his hand, while Oscar was still holding the sheets.

"Look," Oscar said annoyed now that Daniel was telling him what to do, "I will go to breakfast with you and I will see you in Granada in 4 days or so."

"Oh no! You are coming with me. I know your type, you will never get down to Granada and follow your little itinerary to the detail and are not going to have any fun." Daniel pointed to his black journal that was sitting on the desk. "Just go to the places you missed on the way back, you will have to pass through here to get to Lisbon. *Vamos!*" he said and grabbed the travel books and papers from the desk, shoving them in Oscar's backpack.

"*Que no!* I am not going, I will meet you there."

"Well, suit yourself," Daniel said, walking towards the door. "I guess I will have to entertain Monica by myself."

"*Qué?* Monica is going to be here with her sister." All of a sudden Oscar could not contain his secret reason for wanting to stay in the town or vicinities.

"Monica said that as soon as the train strike was off, she was heading home. You have my number, so I will see you around." Daniel shrugged his head as he turned the knob to lock the door behind him.

"Wait, you are right. I am not being adventurous or a good traveller. I will go with you and see these sights upon my return," Oscar said before the door shut.

33

"*Bueno tío*! That is more like it! I will meet you in the lobby," Oscar said. Daniel walked down the hallway smiling.

They met up in the lobby, and Oscar was wearing black shorts with black sandals and a plain white t-shirt.

"I need a *café*," Oscar said, as he shuffled his sandals outside the hostal's entrance.

"*Claro, hombre*," Daniel slapped his shoulder, "follow me." They went straight to the corner bar and ordered breakfast.

Oscar thought about all the food they had eaten the night before and was surprised that it had not made him feel more sober. He hadn't really drunk much at the underground party. Oh, he remembered now. Daniel had ordered some shots of whiskey and pushed everyone into adding them with their hot chocolate. After only wanting to have Daniel shut up, he had given into him and proceeded to take one more as the others cheered him on after he drank the first one so quickly. He had Daniel to thank for his disturbing headache, but he also had met Monica. Oscar knew Daniel's type: it was going to be some good with the bad, but Oscar didn't want to think about that now.

His *café con leche* arrived topped with a perfectly slanted heart-shaped white foam. Last night's white foam had been more *Starry Night*. He nodded his head in respect to the bartenders of this city who took such pride in a common drink.

They each ordered a half baguette with thinly cut *jamón*, and sliced tomatoes sprinkled with salt and olive oil. Oscar removed the *jamón* and saved it for last. With each bite he felt better, and after they settled up their bill, the young men walked side by side, with their backpacks on their backs, looking ready for travel, and headed towards the train station.

It was 10:20 when they arrived, and Oscar watched their backpacks as Daniel went to buy the tickets. There were no fans inside the station, and the air conditioning seemed to be broken because the windows were all cracked open. Oscar had to detach his white shirt from his skin. It was so wet, he could have used it to clean the dirty floors and stained seat he was sitting on.

At 11am the train left and they settled into their seats. The layout of the trains was quite civilized. There were mirror tables on each side of the car with four seats surrounding them. Oscar was by the window, with Daniel across from him. There were passengers already on the train when they embarked, but no one was sitting in the aisle seats that adjoined them. In their wagon they passed by other passengers that had laid magazines, books, phones or laptops on their tables.

"*Quieres jugar?*" Daniel asked taking a wooden box out of his backpack that he was searching through overhead.

Oscar agreed and they passed the first hour playing checkers. Alternating between playing black or red, Daniel always blamed his losses on having the black chips. Oscar was not keeping track of the wins and losses, but was sure that Daniel would have blamed the red chips if it happened that he had lost while using that color.

To mix things up a bit, they kept the chips and used them as money coins when they started playing card games. Daniel showed Oscar how to play Poker and the master became the student in the following hour when Oscar kept beating him. Oscar was thrilled, since he was usually not very lucky in games. It could not have been only the luck of the cards; he was winning one after another. His quick learning skill must have contributed to some of the victories, he thought. Daniel got very frustrated and suggested that they finish one more hand. "Why don't we do winner takes all?" Daniel said out of the blue.

Oscar was surprised at first but understood that almost all of the red and black chips were on his side of the table. They agreed to play 7-Card Stud, winner takes all, for the last round. Oscar looked at his cards as he waited for the last card to show up. He tried containing his lips from curling into a smile and held his breath a little bit while his heart pounded louder.

Daniel anxiously asked, "Okay, so what have you got?"

"You show me first. It is your turn," Oscar said calmly.

"*Vale*," Daniel sighed, rolling his eyes and giving away the status of his cards.

He put his cards down in numerical order and displayed a pair of 3's and 5's.

Oscar smiled now, too excited to contain his winning high. First he laid down a 3 of hearts, then a 4 of hearts, and continued until he showed five continuous cards all red, all hearts. Daniel's eyes got bigger as he saw the Straight Flush.

"*Afortunado en el juego, desafortunado en el amor*," he said dryly.

"Slow down, you said that too quick! What does that mean?" Oscar said, incredulous that Daniel might be challenging the validity of his win.

Daniel reached across the table to shake Oscar's hand, which utterly confused him.

"Oh nothing, it is just a Spanish saying. You know how the Spaniards have a saying for everything?" brushing him aside as if his question did not have importance.

"Not really, this would be the second one I have learned since yesterday. What does this one translate to in English?" Oscar asked feeling forced to doubly inquire.

"It means that since you have been so lucky in the game of luck, you will be unlucky in love." Daniel said this with a straight face, almost as if he had read a law from a handbook.

Oscar felt, all of a sudden, as if he had been cursed. He had never felt lucky, per se, in anything particular, but did not want to be unlucky in love at the cost of being lucky at a mere game of luck. If he were lucky in luck, then he would rather transfer the l word to the love category.

The train slowed down again, but instead of stopping for its standard 6 minutes, it stopped for longer. Those who had not disembarked waited the average time of the other stops, and when that time had expired, started looking around, wondering what was occurring. A ticket man passed by and Oscar overheard another passenger asking what was happening.

He said, "*Nos paramos aquí media hora para el descanso de el conductor y trabajadores.*" The man in the blue and white uniform with the ticket stamper in hand spoke so quickly that Oscar barely understood him.

Daniel translated and told him that they would have half an hour at this station. He stood up and almost hit the ceiling above him, the spikes of his black hair grazing the plastic grey covering.

Oscar took a deep breath off the train, relieved to breathe some fresh air and in need of a change of scenery from the stale environment that had been created over a combination of black and red cards.

VII

The train sped forward passing, through large expanses of open lands with mountains in the far distance. Oscar read his guidebook and started with the description of Extremadura that stated, 'A desolate and sun-parched land that is probably not worth visiting.' What kind of a description is that? He thought. Fascinated by the nothingness, he felt offended that some tour guide or travel critic had written this about his current surroundings.

He went on to read all of the descriptions about this province and finished on the culinary section that highlighted the importance of *pata negra*. This meant black leg, but why was there three pages on this part?

After finishing this lengthy description he realized that *pata negra* was a type of ham that was regarded as the best jamón in Spain.

"Did you know that Extremadura is known for *pata negra?*"

"*Pues claro, hombre!*" Daniel responded without looking away from his book.

Oscar insisted, "Is this what we were eating the whole time at the Cafe Estrella?"

"Yep," he answered.

"I knew that *jamón* tasted so good, but was completely unaware that it was this *pata negra*. Have you seen these pigs, are their legs really black?" Oscar asked.

Daniel looked up from his book and explained, "*Qué sí hombre!* The whole pig is black not only the legs. Some of them could be a dark grey, but the whole animal is dark overall. The reason they are so famous is that they are free to roam around the farms and eat only acorns. Something about that process makes them better tasting than the other bastard pigs. But, don't you Portuguese have this ham too? I am sure you have tasted it in Lisbon?"

Oscar said, "Yes, we have this *jamón*, but we call it Alentejo, and it just did not taste like the *pata negra*."

Oscar continued on and on about the differences in ham, and all this food talk was making him hungry.

The train slowed down and came to a complete stop. Oscar looked around as most passengers got off and it made him anxious that Daniel still had his nose buried in the book and showed no interest in moving or inquiring about their location.

They disembarked the train and looked for a spot in the cafe to have some lunch. The music inside was blasting. If that room had had a choice, it would have been a club instead of a bar. Oscar pointed to a baguette with chorizo and *queso manchego*. The bleached-blond haired, middle-aged woman grabbed it with silver tongs and put it on a plate. Oscar agreed when she asked if he wanted it cut in half.

"*Para beber?*" she asked.

"*Una Coca Cola con hielo, por favor.*" Oscar was proud of his Spanish and spoke slowly so he would be understood.

Blondie smiled when she saw his effort and put an extra lemon in his tall glass before pouring the soda inside of it. Daniel was behind Oscar and ordered the same thing.

They sat in the corner table underneath the speakers that were blasting one of Madonna's new songs, "Nothing Really Matters." It felt like their ears were going to explode. The bass was making their bodies vibrate and Oscar looked up from his *bocadillo* and saw that the other customers were unbothered by the volume. The Spaniards just spoke louder and louder as the song escalated.

"Nothing really matters. Love is all we need. Everything I give you . . . All comes back to me."

The lyrics repeated over and over until they got into Oscar's head and he would not be able to leave them until he arrived in Granada.

The oddest thing happened—a girl, on the other side of the room, was dancing just like the video on the television bolted above her head. She was seesawing her wild, black hair while singing and robotically contorting her arms and hips.

The video finally ended. Madonna's red silk Japanese robe disappeared and was replaced by a Spanish group of rock and rollers singing teen-angst songs with the crowd jumping up and down to their beat. The Madonna dancing girl kept dancing the moves from the previous song matching the new beat. Her friend joined in and they both moved their heads up and down, left and right with brusque movements and curved their backs.

This was quite a show, Oscar thought, for a small cafe on a train stop in a town whose name he still did not know. Daniel was enjoying the show and started copying the girl's movements, making Oscar laugh. His arm movements became more disruptive and Oscar barely caught the Coca Cola glass with his right hand before it dripped all over his lap.

With caffeine in his veins and a renewed energy from the musical performances, Oscar stepped outside to stretch his body.

"So where are we exactly?" Oscar said, while pointing to Granada on a glass-enclosed map.

Daniel started laughing. "*No hombre*! Not that way, we have headed completely eastbound. We are over here." He grabbed Oscar's finger and moved it up and then to the right. "*Aquí*," pointing to a town called Villarobledo.

"We have been travelling for 7 hours already. This is not even on the way!" Oscar exclaimed.

"Sort of, mate. There are no straight train lines to Granada."

"You are killing me! We are travelling all over! How much longer do we have? I thought we were very close to our destination."

"*Más o menos,* you know, more or less, it's really all relative. We are somewhat closer than we started, but farther than what you had anticipated," Daniel said in a teasing voice.

"*No jodas tío*! How much longer, once this train starts again?" Oscar said.

"Ummmm," Daniel said, delaying his answer. "Do you mean how much longer until sundown, are you wanting to know the tilt of the earth or how many degrees in longitude or would that be latitude?"

Oscar made a fist and punched Daniel on the arm, a little harder than he had meant to, but his frustration was growing. He was now afraid that Daniel was going to inform him of a number he did not want to hear.

"Come on, spill it. Is it gonna be the year 2000 before we get there?"

"No, of course not, much before that. Just a few more hours, you know, like 5 or so," Daniel said waiting for his reaction. "We can see 2000 in a few months. We'll see Granada much before that."

"What exactly are we going there for? Please remind me." Oscar should have taken a better look at the map and not depended on Daniel for instruction. It seemed to him that Daniel was a trickster and enjoyed playing jokes on people.

"To party and also for your...Gu..gu..gu..girl...friend," Daniel said in a mocking tone.

Oscar felt embarrassed at the mention of Monica as his girlfriend. What if she had not even given him the right number? What if he was being rushed around Spain with no other reason than to please Daniel and his compulsive ideas?

Oscar realized that the first part of his trip had been spent in such a gambling frenzy that he had not noticed the village names that were heading them directly East instead of South. He grabbed his travel book. Finding Badajoz easily, he saw how much closer to home this was than his current location. After having Daniel spell out the village they had just departed, he found it in the Castilla-La Mancha region of Spain. Going to the index he found the pages that described this area, and he learned that this was the setting for Miguel Cervantes' *Don Quijote*. Oscar was in the middle of a masterpiece. It was probably more in the nothing that Cervantes must have found inspiration. The area was sparsely populated and when something appeared in view it was usually one of the hundreds of olive trees or vineyards. The grapes must be suffering adequately as the earth beneath the vines seemed to have forgotten the taste of water and only knew its taker, the sun. The earth was so parched that it appeared white, bleached from the sun, and on the horizon there was a thick white pillow of heat that was preventing the sun from reaching the earth.

Oscar smiled and got closer to the window when the row of windmills appeared. There were ten, twenty, maybe more, rolling up and down the hills, with their faces spinning in the flow of the air.

Oscar realized that for the first time he was appreciating his environment and grew excited when he found a castle in the distance, imagining Medieval warriors climbing the hills ready for their next conquest. Swords swiftly drawn, ready for death. As the train gripped sharply to the turn, another castle appeared. There was a large indentation around it, perhaps once a moat. It seemed incredible that water could live in this dry land; Oscar looked around for signs of water, but found none.

Four perfectly spaced towers framed the main entrance of the castle. Oscar imagined knights on horses with royalty stiffly standing in red and gold. The children would bring the knights flowers, honoring them for their victories. The trumpets and violin music would echo the walls, and the notes would reach the clouds.

What was Oscar's interesting story? He felt humbled by this architectural wonder. His background seemed too blasé, so common, so lacking in adventure. These warriors had fought and travelled to defend their lands and kings. The most Oscar had done was get on a train with his map secured to his arm like a safety blanket and then felt out of control when his plans had changed.

Maybe this was what travelling was about. Finding places he was not supposed to find, going on unplanned routes. He felt happiness in this thought, but also felt an inferiority to those soldiers. Those metal warriors had travelled these dry lands on foot, not in the comfort and protection of a vehicle whose steel coverings were used to shield him from the elements, from the heat and make his travel smooth and, most importantly of all, disengaging.

If he were to get off on the next stop and walk towards this castle, arrive to it, climb its broken stairs and reach one of the openings in the facade, prop himself through it with legs dangling, would that not be when he truly had a righteous view, instead of being the simplistic onlooker who gazed as he passed, but felt nothing but an urge to get his camera and record what others had done, giving himself some rewarding feeling for doing something like taking a picture? Could the camera really capture what had occurred here? Most likely not. It arrived too late, when the wars had already been fought, the blood spread on the stones, the illusions lost, the tiredness from lack of sleep had already been given its rest, and the thirst had been quenched by death or drink.

A triple beep on his cell phone interrupted his "historical vision" of place and brought him back to the present moment in time. He flipped up his phone thinking and hoping that it was perhaps Monica, but it was not. It was a female, with one less letter in her name, his sister, Elena. He realized that it could not be Monica because she did not have his number and he had been distracted and never written to her in the first place, thus, a respond was impossible.

Elena's text message greeted him with exclamations and happy faces inquiring about his trip, how it was going, was he enjoying himself? Four questions followed each other with a range of punctuation marks used freely and often.

He could sense her excitement, and he wrote back, making sure to include lots of exclamations so his return message would prove to be satisfactory in her heart.

"I am lost in the fields of Castilla-La Mancha! This is the land of Don Quijote, which I read so many years ago. The castles are enormous and the lands are dry, filled with olive trees and vineyards!!!" he texted.

Elena wrote back, "Fantastic!!! All is good at home. Mom is complaining like always but I have had a good time, there was a beach party I went to and I was back home before the parents realized that I had snuck out. :-) They texted back and forth, and he put his phone down when Elena said goodbye.

Oscar thought of Monica again. If he called her and said he was on his way to Granada she might think he was too eager. Knowing his luck, she was probably still in Badajoz. What if he sent her a text? That would seem less intrusive and that way she could answer on her own time.

After some erasing of words, and restructuring, he settled on the following:
"On the train with Dani, heading to your homeland, Granada. This is my number, text me if you would like to meet."

After pressing Send, he began to doubt the quality of that text. He started questioning why he had written, "if you would like to meet." Instead of something more welcoming, meaning he would like to see her. He tortured his brain for 20 more minutes and decided to clear his mind by reading the magazine so he would not keep hammering himself at his poor choice of words.

The travel magazine he had bought had an article in it regarding a town in Almeria. He instantly went to his Guidebook to see if he would be passing this region, but the village in question, Palomares, was on the coast and still further east than Granada. Perhaps he would travel there next. The thought comforted his brain with a new idea of freedom of choice.

A beep, beep, beep on his phone interrupted his reading. A text appeared and he figuratively crossed his fingers hoping that it was Monica.

"Just arrived to Granada, *tanto calor*! Where are you now?" Monica wrote.

Oscar could not believe she was already there. Daniel must have taken them on the route for idiots around all of the country. Wait! He thought, he wasn't going to let that bother him. It was fine, he reassured himself, he would not have seen the beautiful castles if they had not wandered through these parts of Castilla-La Mancha. Waiting a few minutes to not seem anxious, he texted back, "Just asked a gentleman and he said we are two hours away. Are you free tonight?"

After sending the text, he wondered if it was too much, since they would be arriving close to 8pm. He had not appeared very interested in his first messages, so this would clear any previous doubts.

She responded with the following, "Have some family events tonight, perhaps another day."

Oscar wrote, "I will call you tomorrow and we can see what works later this week." She answered back with a happy face and her name—Monica. He just loved seeing it written. It was such a beautiful, mysterious-sounding name, both friendly and dark. He had always liked that name.

VIII

It was still daylight as the train pushed on. The sun was not setting until 10pm, each night a few minutes earlier. Daniel was lost in his book. The motion of the train slowed down and Oscar nudged Daniel to indicate they were arriving.

"Where are we staying?" Oscar asked, thinking he should have discussed this earlier on in the trip, in case there was a discussion needed about it.

"Don't worry about it," Daniel responded, still not looking up from his book. This answer actually made Oscar worry more, since he realized he did not know Daniel very well at all. The wheels of the train made a whistling sound and Oscar felt the excitement of getting off this odyssey of a train trip.

Suddenly, two uniformed men approached him. "Oscar Santos?" they said in a firm voice. "*Sí*," he responded. "*Venga con nosotros. Eres sospechoso y le tenemos que interrogar en la estación,*" they said very quickly. Oscar turned around to look at Daniel. "What are they saying?"

Daniel translated, "You are a suspect and we are taking you to the police station to question you. They are asking you to go with them." Daniel started hassling them, explaining that there must have been a misunderstanding, finally getting a bit physical, pushing on one of the Guardia's shoulders.

"*No seas un chuleta!*" the policeman told Daniel. Oscar asked Daniel, "What did he say?" Daniel responded, "Basically don't be an asshole."

The exchange in English was irritating the policemen, which Daniel explained were "Guardia Civil," a type of military police.

Oscar explained in his best Spanish that he had not done anything wrong, taking out his passport from his backpack, which he had thankfully brought, even though travelling within the European Union made it unnecessary.

The military policeman grabbed Oscar's arm with force, and this was not to Daniel's liking as he yelled at him to let him go.

Within ten minutes, Daniel and Oscar had been transferred from the comfort of their cramped train seats to a police car's back seats.

Oscar looked down at his handcuffs in disbelief. The young men talked about the ridiculousness of this situation. Daniel curiously asked Oscar if he was wanted in Portugal. "Of course not," Oscar responded.

Oscar was sweating now. Apart from the lack of air conditioning in the back seat, he was emotionally jigsawed and did not know how to put himself back together. He had never done anything that exciting or dangerous to be reprimanded and subjugated to handcuffs.

The car's temperature would prove to be mild compared to the heat of the police station. They both sat on blue chairs staring at beige chipping paint for over an hour. They speculated about the reasons for their arrest.

Their hunger led them to talk about food and relive last night's banquet. Then Daniel asked, "If you were going to be electrocuted tomorrow, what would your last meal be?"

"Wow! I hope that doesn't happen to us. You are making me think of the Last Supper or something like that. I don't know, I guess it would have to be something I can usually never eat, or maybe it would be my favorite food. Let me think. In Portugal we have this rice dish similar to the Spanish paella but ours is spicy and how my grandmother makes it is better than any restaurant in Lisbon I have ever tasted. However, the thought of bringing my grandmother to prison is a sad thought, and if that is the last thing she did before she died, you know, cook her only grandson some rice, then it would seem like a morbid final act."

Daniel said, "Oh, I remember that rice dish when we went to Portugal. I was the only one of my entire family that liked it. Nobody else likes spicy food and as typical Spaniards most everyone said that the Spanish version was superior. *Típico*! My father is British, so he has no sense of a culinary palate, and don't you worry, my mother never failed to remind him of that. Unfortunately, our time in Portugal may have been one of our last family vacations. I guess, it is all for the better, since they were fighting so much."

Oscar tried to lighten the mood, "It seems that I would be stuck eating a poor version of the spicy rice, cooked by some Granadino, who would probably change it to the Spanish paella, just to spite me! Not being granted your last dying wish! What a slap in the face! And you Daniel, what would your last supper be?"

"There are these artichokes called *carciofi alla giudia*, basically poor Jewish artichokes, but a Roman girl at the university made them for us and I have never tasted a better vegetable. Am I allowed more than one plate?"

"Sure," Oscar responded. "As good Spaniards, they would probably offer a *primero, segundo* and *postre*. Kind of like a "*Menú del Día.*"

This made both of them laugh and they imagined their requested menu written in white chalk on a black board near the entryway of a café or restaurant.

"Let's see. For second plate I would get a filet mignon, with double baked salted potatoes and fresh chives and sour cream. And for dessert a cheesecake with strawberries and Pop Rocks sprinkled on top!"

"What was the last thing you said?" Oscar asked, trying to imagine this last strange request.

Daniel smiled, "One time in London we went to this funky restaurant and ate this cheesecake, you know, the Americans love that stuff. This was one trendy-looking place with lots of neon green and pink. I think it was my sister's idea. Anyway, this cheesecake was topped with fresh strawberries and dark chocolate syrup and placed on this long narrow plate and one side was the cheesecake and on the other the syrup trailed on top of fresh whipped cream sprinkled with Pop Rocks. It looked like a tail or something coming out of the back of the cheesecake. So it sounds crazy and all that, but once you bit into it there was an explosion in your mouth, and combined with the sweetness of the cheese cake, the crunch of the slightly unripened strawberries, there was basically a party in your mouth."

"Delicious," Oscar said, hungrier than ever.

Daniel continued, "Talking about sweet stuff, one time my sister Clarabel and I tried making ice cream. It was a complete disaster. I mean, you would think that it was simply putting milk and ice, fruit or some nuts and mixing it up. Oh no! There was rock salt involved and we kept trying to eat it through the whole process. We made such a mess we were almost banished from the kitchen, but Mum realized that she needed us to help feed so many people, so the banishment was just relegated to ice cream making."

Oscar thought about what strange things he and Elena had made in the kitchen, but could not think of anything. It seemed that Daniel always had stories to tell. Oscar questioned his own sense of storytelling and made a note to try to think of more interesting stories from his life. Was it that he did not tell stories as well as Daniel, or had his life been simpler, typical or just plain boring with nothing to tell? Before he could ponder this some more, Daniel was off telling another funny story.

"Did I tell you that my parents named us all so that our names would end in L? What kind of a preposterous idea is that?"

"So what are all the names?" Oscar asked, searching through his heads for names ending in the letter l.

"So, apart from Daniel and Clarabel," he started rolling the l to make it more apparent, "there are Joel, Gabriel and Laurel.

"Laurel got the worst of it. You see, in England her name sounds cool, but here in Spain they take a big piss about it, because it is an herb that the Spaniards use in everything! So in school especially, the kids make fun of her when they first hear it. When she was young it was really hard, but now when she travels everyone in other countries thinks it is cool, so she feels vindicated for this strange choice by my parents.

"So Oscar, I was just thinking that you have never told me what you do. I know you finished the university and all that, but after these travels, what next?"

"I finished with a degree in anthropology so once I return, I will start looking for a job, I guess," Oscar explained.

"What in the world do you do with anthropology, get a hammer and start looking for fossils?" Daniel asked with surprise.

"I guess you could do that, but you wouldn't use a hammer. That portion is actually known as archeology. Let me explain. There are various types of anthropology, but the one I specialized in is cultural anthropology. This is basically the study of the culture of early man, discovering what his social life was like, his interaction with others, the use of language and customs. The idea is to create a model of what culture was like for him, and her, of course. The archeologist finds artifacts beneath the surface of the Earth, where our ancient civilization previously lived. The idea is to create a story to show how we used to live, interact with each other and with nature. The story is cultural anthropology, and the plot and characters are dug up by archeology, both figuratively and literally."

Daniel got an idea, "Wicked, it sounds like you are totally into this. I'm surprised you did not mention it before."

"We have only known each other for 24 hours." Oscar looked down at his watch and realized that it was just over the 24 hours when he stepped into the train station in Badajoz, now seeming a lifetime away.

Daniel had continuing curiosity about Oscar's choice of studies. "Now wait a second, what made you study anthropology or archeology or whatever you call it?"

Oscar looked away a bit. "Actually, well, this is going to sound a bit, strange, I guess, but when I was younger I saw the Indiana Jones movie and I thought it would be a fun job to have. Ok, don't make fun of me, super cliché, I know, but it is what brought the inspiration to study this field. The reality is that most of the time in actual archeology in the field is spent tediously removing dirt, cleaning a small piece of bone or fragment for hours to then spend the other hours researching and classifying your finds. After that you try to put it all together, and do some more research. There is not really a part where you put on a hat and use whips to keep the bad guys away. I have not yet seen hidden maps or an x to mark the spot."

They continued reenacting the Indiana Jones scenes they most liked and got caught up in the stories until the guard had to repeat for the third time, "*Vamos!*"

It was time to go, but they did not know their destination. They left the small station still in handcuffs and were placed in a bus that seemed to be leaving the city.

"What the fuck is going on?" Daniel yelled at the policemen in front of the car.

"*Tranquilo!*" They instructed him to calm down, which did quite the opposite. He jumped up and down in his seat as much as he could, considering the lack of movement from being handcuffed in front and tied down by a seatbelt. That had been very thoughtful of them to strap them in with a seatbelt. Oscar wondered if convicted murderers were given such delicate treatment.

IX

They reached a new location 20 minutes later and were escorted from the car by two men twice or thrice their size in width, but not in stature. Daniel's Spanish was obviously better, so he tried for the umpteenth time to explain that this had all been a misunderstanding. They were not guilty of anything besides a bad attitude, and this, in itself, was not punishable by law. He threw down technical words, confusingly arranging sentences, which made Oscar's brain spin and gave him no clarity to Daniel's point.

They went inside and were taken through hallways that went right, then left, then right again, to the point that they felt so deep into this building that had they had their handcuffs taken off and been set free, they still would not know how to escape the room they were finally placed in.

Either the light on the table was blindingly bright, or the black walls created a stark contrast that made the lamp's energetic reflection difficult to look towards. Regardless of which it was, Oscar felt very scared for the first time since the arrest. He was separated from Daniel and in that instance felt separated from the world.

The Guardia Civil began the interrogation with personal identity questions. It would have been more comfortable in his native Portuguese, but Oscar tried to avoid getting nervous and asked them to repeat the technical questions. There were words he did not know, but why would he? He had never been in a Spanish jail before.

"Señor Santos, cual es la intención de su visita a nuestro país?"

"*Perdón, mas lento,*" Oscar said, partly because he wasn't sure of the question and also to buy time.

"My intention of travel was simply that, to see a new country. As you can see I have never travelled outside of Portugal, so whomever you are confusing me with, I am not him."

The most difficult thing was that even though it was obvious in Oscar's mind that this misunderstanding was just a simple confusion of persons, it made him nervous to think what this "other" Oscar Santos must have done.

"Can you please tell me what I am accused of? What is it that you think I have done?" he pleaded.

The policeman avoided his question and shuffled through the papers in the thick file. Documents were extracted, read, and shoved back. The pressure on Oscar to confess became intolerable.

"*Avocato,*" burst out of Oscar's mouth.

"You want a lawyer, Son? Well that is going to take a while before we get one."

Silence fell between the two men until Oscar was left alone in the dark room, staring at the light and realizing the room had no windows and no way to escape.

A half hour passed or an hour, it was hard to tell. They had taken his watch, cell phone and all personal belongings and placed them in a box before he'd entered this dark room.

Suddenly, he heard a lot of noise outside his door and what seemed to be a familiar voice.

Daniel was brought in, still with handcuffs. At this point it was just for dramatic effect, since they could not go anywhere in these windowless rooms. Daniel was smiling. Oscar could not believe it–what must have occurred? Smiling was the last thing Oscar felt like doing.

"*No te preocupes*, I am here," Daniel said with a big smirk on his face.

Daniel started speaking quickly to the policemen and, after more interaction that Oscar could not understand, the officers went to each of them and took off the handcuffs.

This was positive, Oscar thought, we are progressing towards freedom.

"What did you say to them?" Oscar really wanted to know.

"*Nada hombre*. I explained to them that by Code 13, we are entitled to freedom of physical restraint until enough evidence has been predetermined against us." More technical information continued and Oscar all of a sudden felt as if he were with a different person. Where was the Daniel he knew? Well "knew" seemed like a strong word, since they had not reached 48 hours, but the Daniel in front of him spoke like a lawyer, and that was the last thing he imagined that he was.

"Don't look so confused, it is all going to be fine. Put your trust in me." Daniel smiled with his Joker expression, which to Oscar did not look trustworthy. It wasn't a used-car-salesman type of look, as much as a look of someone who was going to take you skydiving, push you off a plane, when they knew you didn't have a parachute. Oscar felt uncertain. Why was Daniel talking so differently now?

The policemen kept speaking only to Daniel now and Oscar felt no need to be there since he appeared to be invisible in their eyes.

Again they left Oscar alone and after a time lapse, which he could no longer quantify, they escorted him out of the dark room, through hallways with neon lights, some flashing because they needed replacement and into a silence that was interrupted only by the distant sound of somebody rattling an object sideways through the jail cell steel bars, as if they were playing a harp.

They were given back their belongings, made to sign more paperwork and were then led out the two main doors that were extremely heavy to push but quick to close behind them, nearly snapping Daniel's fingers.

The damp sweaty air and Scirocco winds blanketed over their bodies, and Oscar reminded himself to take a deep breath as his heart attempted to pound out of his body.

Without realizing it, they both jumped up at the same time with hands in the air, shouting out the biggest sigh of relief and planting feet back down on the ground simultaneously.

"What the fuck was that all about?" "What did you tell them? It sounded like Latin to me, were you speaking a different language?"

"*Tranquilo*, I will explain," Daniel said confidently as he held open the door and like something out of a movie, graciously welcomed him into the police car with a gesture of his hand as if he were the chauffeur and they were going to an elegant party.

The police car drove back mainly in the dark until they reached the lighted area and in these twenty minutes or so Daniel explained something about himself.

"I studied law, you see, when I was at the University of Madrid. Today I could have been an upright citizen, maybe even a big shot lawyer in the city, but that is not how it all worked out."

"Ok, so HOW did it all work out?" Oscar inquired.

"Well, it is a big complicated," Daniel started and then stopped.

"Try me!" Oscar said, incredulous that they had been through all this and now Daniel was getting shy about telling his story.

"So university was a blast. Best time of my life, so much fun, so much partying, women, oh, and the learning part was brilliant too. Law came naturally to me, and I started focusing on criminology. After taking some psychology courses for my science requirement, I thought up of different ways to commit "Little" crimes and see if I could get away with them. I wasn't really harming anybody, not killing anybody or anything like that, but I wanted to see how the justice system worked and be inside of it, instead of just studying it in a dusty library. So I got a bit in trouble finally." Daniel paused for dramatic effect, then continued after 30 seconds.

"I don't have the stomach to kill anybody or even hurt an animal, but robbery, now that seemed to be interesting to me, the killing of somebody's goods or material possessions. The whole idea of ownership fascinates me and also kills my spirit. So what could I steal that would be interesting? I thought about it long and hard and realized that intellectual property would be a challenge. Somehow and in some way our upcoming exam ended up in my hands."

"Before everything was so electronic as it is today, Professors actually had exams that were written on paper, stored in their briefcases and all that good stuff. So I went to visit my professor for my Criminological Theory class. His name was Profesor Emilio Cano Cruz. Wickedly smart guy, but organizationally a mess. His office looked like the remnants of a hurricane. Books spilling out of their shelves, stacks of papers all over the desk and the floor. No space was undecorated, as notes hung taped on the lamp and the walls had sticky notes with reminders to do this and that alongside photos of criminal-looking men in between framed diplomas and awards. My intention was to find the final exam that would take place the following week. Profesor Cruz was called to the door by another student, and I knew this was my only chance. I faked dropping my notebook on the floor, reached into his briefcase and fingered through until I found what looked like the exam. There were several copies, with red markings. It was hard to figure out which one was the most recent, but I took one of the ones in the middle. My heart was beating to a techno song at an underground club, my hands were sweating, I had never felt that nervous and exhilarated at the same time.

"When he returned I was lying flat under his desk, with exam in hand and notebook in another, but shielded from his eye's view because of the fortress of books and papers surrounding the desk.

60

"'*Que pasa hombre?*' he asked, with a confused look as if I were doing pushups underneath his desk, since I was moving up and down.

"'*Nada,*' I responded and proceeded to make up the story that my notebook had fallen and I had knocked down one of his stacks of papers and told him 'What a mess you have here, how could you find anything?'

"He returned an apologetic answer, nodding his head in agreeance as I proceeded to inform him of techniques to keep a tidy workplace. He continued his nodding accustomed to the reprimands as if he were a child agreeing with his parents.

"I started an elaborate question-and-answer session. I knew the answers would have lengthy responses and I wrote notes as he spoke. When I could tell he was growing exhausted, I informed him that I was due for another class and thanked him for his time. You could tell he was proud of himself because my questions had become more complex as he explained, only possible if he was doing a good job of explaining, and he gave himself credit for my effective comprehension.

"It didn't seem fair to keep the key of answers to myself, so I used my entrepreneurial spirit and made a little business of taking from the rich to give to the poor—essentially me. I didn't mind sharing outrageous fees, to these '*Hijos de papa,*' you know, the rich kids who are studying at the University because their parents make them, and are occupying space and taking oxygen with no good reason. They had jobs waiting for them once they completed these four or five years. Their presence was no more welcomed to me than a leech on my skin, but without them my growing business would have failed, so I was half-thankful for them for giving me a discretionary income.

"The board of directors became suspicious when all of a sudden there was a much higher average grade in all the law courses within the last six months. Through trial and error, they figured out the students whose grades had dramatically bettered in the last few months. Mine had always been at the top tier, but now they were perfect scores. I had originally intended to do this just once for the high, for the adventure of being a thief, but had not realized how addicting this thiefdom was, so I had continued too long and became greedy, creating an evident pattern that finally led the university to sit me down at the Dean's office, surrounded by a board of angry-looking men.

"Because I had burned all evidence, there was no legal way to prove it had been me. Yes, other students had finally tattled under pressure, but their word was just hearsay. All transactions had been in cash and the original stolen tests could not be found. I was tempted to keep them, I will be honest, there is a high and feeling of propriety with taken items, but I did not want to fall into that trap of, you know, evidence, but I will tell you that I do understand the mind of criminals and why they so enjoy the process of keeping personal items from their victims."

Oscar wanted to know the next part. "So what happened after that? Did they get you to confess under pressure? Were you expelled?"

Daniel spoke in a proud voice, "Considering the nature of the school, they knew very well, that without hard legal proof, they could not prosecute me, so I continued on to graduate with very high scores and completed my law degree."

"This must have outraged them!" Oscar said loudly, forgetting they were still in the police car, but now was able to raise his hands towards his head with the absence of the handcuffs.

"Well you can imagine," Daniel started calmly. "After that I realized that doing the lawyer thing, in the courtroom, and all that was not for me, that eventually I would tire of it and become a criminal myself from boredom."

"So, now what? Are you going to study something else? If you are not an official registered lawyer, what will you do?" Oscar expressed concern in his voice.

Daniel did not seem concerned in the least. "This experience ended up being positive, by showing me how easy to manipulate the system was, and actually is, and how it screams to be broken, to see if its laws stand the test of time. The law and the institution of man (because it has usually always been man, not woman) and the imposition of 'the law' is really what separates us from the animals. That we want to commit crimes, steal, be destructive is what bonds us to animals, but the thought of wanting to control these tendencies is what makes us differ from them."

Oscar sat in silence thinking about how much this all made sense to him. The radio beeped for help intermittently and the car drove on surrendering to the inconsistencies of the pavement.

Daniel continued his monologue, "All this philosophical thought of the law and the idea of meeting criminals, defending them, or being on the other side and trying to convict them, well, this just seemed to me to be an existence of pushing papers, going on technicalities, loop holes, and after my experience with how I had broken the law so simply and gotten away with it, I figured out that this was not the career for me. I yearn to be where the action is, see the crimes occurring, following the presumed guilty, or guilty-to-be and get in the night scene where all the "good" stuff happens. All this being said is what led me to my new occupation."

"And... What is that, what good alternative did you find to being a respectable lawyer?" Oscar asked, not sure why Daniel did not just tell him, but then realized that Daniel liked provoking Oscar's curiosity.

"So I became a detective. It is really the best fit for me, anyways, and I am glad I went through all of that to have the freedom I have today. You see, I can make my own hours, choose the cases I want to work on, and do it on my own time. Yes, I have to follow the laws that are placed by the judicial system, but it is more flexible, let's say, because I won't get my law license taken away if I don't do things exactly by code. People that hire me are doing it in a private agreement, what they are willing to pay me to do is again, private and confidential."

Oscar felt himself to be a boring creature compared to Daniel's exciting life as a private detective. His mind thought of famous detectives of the past, Sherlock Holmes, Miss Marple, Inspector Clouseau, even Jessica Fletcher, from "Murder She Wrote" had more interesting lives than what he foresaw in his future of cleaning dusty bones. This risky detective career seemed full of adventures. Perhaps his archeology choice would bring him storybook and Hollywood-like adventures, but at this moment he felt that it was just in his imagination.

"Why didn't you do all this explaining when we were downtown inside the cell, instead of waiting for the maximum security jail?" Oscar asked.

Daniel brushed him off, "Don't exaggerate, that one was not maximum security. You obviously have not been around the jails too much!"

"NOR do I want to be," Oscar interrupted his explanation.

Daniel proceeded, "Look, it's not that I wanted to take it to another level, we were having such an interesting conversation on anthropology, astrology and everything else you like and studied, that I was enjoying myself, forgetting that we were in handcuffs."

"I did not forget!" Oscar insisted. "You kept asking me more questions, but I did not forget that we were handcuffed in a jail in Granada! This has not happened to me before. By the confidence of your demeanor through these parts, I am having a feeling that this is not your first time."

Oscar continued while he had a chance, "And let's set things straight, I was not talking about astrology, I was explaining archeology." Oscar felt it was necessary to clarify this difference.

"*Bueno, a lo hecho, pecho!*" Daniel laughed.

"What does that mean? Is this one of your Spanish sayings?" He was having a feeling that the Spaniards love to have little sayings about everything, or perhaps it was only Daniel that said them so often.

"It means to what you have done, *chest*." He laughed at himself, because it didn't seem to make any sense. "Well, what it actually means is, 'We must accept the choices we have made, and move onward.'"

Oscar sighed, "Do you realize that after all of these stories and sayings, you still have not told me why we were arrested?"

"Oh, right. There is some other Oscar Santos from the Basque country suspected of terrorism. This area is in the north and they are famous for having separatist groups who plant car bombs. I explained to the Guardia Civil that you were obviously not a Spaniard as you would have recognized *pata negra jamón* as soon as you tasted it, so they let us go."

Oscar could not contain his laughter and happy tears nearly ran down his face. He punched Daniel and they wrestled in the back seat until the driver told them to settle down. When they straightened up in their seats, a magically lit castle stood before them. The architecture was decidedly different from the castles Oscar had seen in the land of Don Quixote. The towers were square with unique key-shaped windows and a central tower stood above the colossal fortress. Beyond the castle, the sun cast its final glow as the moon gleamed above the imposing mountains.

"La Alhambra," Daniel pointed.

Curving around this spectacle, the police car weaved through the streets and finally came to a stop. The policemen asked if they had all their documentation and after confirming that they did, Daniel saluted the two officers and said *"Gracias por este tour de Granada!"* Oscar understood he had just thanked them for taking them on a tour of Granada, and the sarcasm in Daniel's voice could have been understood even by a non-Spanish speaker.

The cop nodded his head, *"Mira que cachondeo que tienes, hijo."*

Daniel grabbed Oscar's arm and hooked around it marching with his legs high up in the air singing. "*Un, dos tres, derecha, derecha, derecha, izquierda, derecha.*"

"What was that?" Oscar asked, overjoyed to be out of the car, but wondering if Daniel maybe deserved to be put back in. He was unaware, that he was now marching alongside Daniel.

"Don't you understand, One, two, three, left, right, left."

"No, idiot, what did the officer say to you?" Oscar continued, knowing that Daniel was joking some more and as always, making him ask several times to increase the dramatic effect.

"He said that I had a brilliant sense of humor, had enjoyed taking us around this marvelous city, wished us the best and reminded me not to take any more exams from the university professors."

Oscar finally escaped Daniel's side grip. "Seriously, *hombre*, what did he say to you?"

Daniel smiled and gave in. "All right, he said that I had a lot of *cachondeo*. This word means 'sarcastic humor.' *Jodiendo un poco. Sin querer, queriendo.* The officer thought I was a smartass."

"Shocking," Oscar appropriately responded. "Well, I am just glad that they didn't arrest us again for insulting a law officer. I am starting to get a feeling that you must have been in trouble with the law at other points in your life. As for me, this was my first time in a cop car and I hope the last."

Daniel had to put his two cents in, "But think of what a good travel anecdote that will make in your journal; I hope to provide a new experience, a breaking from your virginal inclinations."

Daniel's smirk was so mischievous that Oscar interrupted him now. "Ok, I don't want to hear all about your conquests, what I want to know is if our resting place is close. I am ready for a *cerveza* and a shower. Aren't you exhausted?"

"Not really! My mind is just waking up!" Daniel said, still looking as though he was not up to anything good.

X

Daniel pointed, "That way, we are almost there. It's at the end of that street, on the right."

"*Esta es*," Daniel said getting his keys from the front flap of his backpack.

Although his movements were slow and controlled, Daniel was unable to silence the old locks he was turning, since they required four rotating clicks to open each key hole, three in total. Click, clonk, click, the stone floors echoing each turn of his wrist, Oscar figured that they would wake up the whole apartment building. The hallways were completely silent except for the key's undoings.

Oscar felt like a thief in the night, an intruder. Going to somebody's house at this hour seemed inappropriate, but his body quieted his mind as he thought of lying down, finally horizontal.

Daniel put his finger to his mouth, signaling Oscar not to speak, and they stepped softly down a narrow hallway, and after closing the door behind them, Daniel turned on a light with a string, and Oscar adjusted his eyes to see two low twin beds in an L shape with a small desk and shelves filled with books above it. He searched through his toiletry bag and found his toothpaste and toothbrush. Daniel instructed him to be quiet and to turn left for the bathroom. Oscar nodded his head.

The bathroom was also very small with a toilet, bidet, and sink with a mirror above. He started the shower, undressed from his white boxer shorts, and stepped into the cold paradise. He closed his eyes at first as the cold water massaged his head. When he opened his eyes, he saw his body looked much more tanned than he expected; it must have been the contrast with the white mosaic tiles.

The thought of waking up Daniel's mother brought him out of the waterfall and he opened up the white wooden cabinet and found a white towel. The drawers below were bursting with bottles, creams and sprays for any body part that could be moisturized and improved. He probably should have asked Daniel first, but the temptation was too strong and he investigated all of the small storage compartments.

He could not help himself from spritzing some Nenuco baby cologne. He remembered this from his little cousins in Lisbon, and the scent was the epitome of clean.

He turned off the bathroom light and instantly regretted it as he walked through the darkness, barely finding his north by the thin ray of light at the bottom of the door. Tiptoeing in, he found Daniel lying down in his underwear.

"Buen idea macho," Daniel said and went to the bathroom again, this time to copy Oscar and take a shower.

Oscar felt a sense of relief, and was glad that it had inspired rather than bothered Daniel. Seconds separated sleep from wake as Oscar's body touched the bed, wet hair melted into the pillow and a steady breath accompanied his dreams.

XI

Oscar did not have a watch close to him when he awoke so he was unsure of the time, but by the brightness of the light and heat in the room, he figured it was past mid-day.

"*Buenos dias!*" Daniel popped his head through the door. "Or should I say *Bom dia, portugues?*" exaggerating the final syllable. Oscar smiled and sat up in the bed. "Get dressed and come eat breakfast! You must be starving, mate," Daniel said eagerly.

Oscar dressed quickly with the first shirt and shorts he found, not giving a care as to whether they matched or not.

When he fully opened the door the smell of bacon overcame him and he remembered how famished he really was and his keen like of pork products.

Oscar let his nose follow the scent, and he arrived in the kitchen where there was a radio playing pop music. He sat down and Daniel served him a plate.

"Did you cook all of this?" Oscar asked with surprise, viewing the seven different items that had been thrown on the plate.

"No, my mom did. She went to buy more bread because I finished the first *barra*," Daniel explained between bites of his second helping.

Oscar did not know where to start. There were baked beans drenched in sauce, cut up potatoes in a triangle shape with parsley sprinkled on top next to three sausage links flanked by two strips of bacon. Some healthier choices were found in the sautéed mushrooms, also with parsley on top and tomatoes that seemed grilled or toasted, a method of cooking he had never seen before. He was used to seeing them fresh in a salad or smashed up in a sauce, but not served this way.

His fork led him to the sausage and he forcefully cut a piece and shoved it in his mouth. The next pieces he ate without regard of their large size and found some eggs underneath the bacon links that had now become infused with the baked bean sauce.

This looked nothing like the Portuguese cuisine he was accustomed to and he would have probably been turned off from such a mess on a plate in most circumstances, had his hunger not overtaken any sense of aesthetic presence on a ceramic plate.

He washed the breakfast down with two cups of coffee and finally started slowing down when he felt his stomach heavy, and with a slight pain from eating so quickly.

Oscar found ice cubes in the freezer and filled up the largest glass he could find in the cupboard to quench his salty mouth. A woman walked in at that very moment and started laughing. *"Pero eso es para poner plantas hijo."*

"Sorry, that is a small vase for flowers, I did not notice you had grabbed that," Daniel said.

Oscar set it down, embarrassed to be drinking water out of a vase and eating in a kitchen whose owner he had not met.

"*No pasa nada. Bebe, tendras sed, con el calor que hace aquí,*" the woman said.

"My mom said it is fine, just drink, we know how hot it is here. I imagine it is more difficult to understand her. She has a very strong accent from Granada," Daniel explained.

Her smile was identical to Daniel's. Wrinkles from sun and smoke lined her beautiful face. The overflowing ashtrays, more full than empty, revealed her habit.

Daniel said, "Let me introduce you to my mum, Alejandra."

"*Mucho gusto,*" she said as she lit up a cigarette.

"This is Oscar, my friend from Portugal," Daniel said with an open palm presenting Oscar, in his typical theatrical tendency. To call him a friend after only two days may have seemed a bit exaggerated, but after all they had been through, it seemed appropriate. He could not recall a friend at home who had taken him so many kilometers in such little time and brought him to see the insides of the jail and one of the wonders of the world all on the same night.

"*Ah, Portuges?*" she said. "*Como se dice, 'mucho gusto' en portuges?*" she questioned Oscar on the proper greeting in his language.

Oscar responded, happy for her interest, "*Muito prazer.*"

Alejandra tried saying it and in typical fashion made the u in the Muito word much deeper than was accurate. "*Bueno,* good job," Oscar said. She smiled again and went out of the kitchen.

73

Daniel offered more food, but Oscar raised his hand in a stop.

"So I did not know that Spaniards ate this kind of breakfast. Is this something typical of Granada?" Oscar asked.

Daniel smiled, "No, this is my father's fault. My mom learned to cook this mess because he always missed it from home and then my siblings and I grew to like it. Considering how much you love *jamón*, I figured you would love bacon and sausage."

Oscar did not want to think of all the pork and other mix of foods that lay in his stomach.

"The beauty of the pork is that it is a centerpiece of Spain's national identity. The idea of Spain was formed with the Reconquista. Sure, the Moors left us the irrigation systems, the strong fortresses and other innovations but as is common in history, you love what your enemy hates. The Spaniards took the pig and elevated it onto a high platter, literally. *Los moros* left nice buildings and a new found love for pig, the dirty animal no one wanted. Popular passion for pork products. It's a tongue twister, huh?"

Without waiting for an answer, he continued. "As you can tell our whole family loves the pig for different reasons, but these breakfasts are not served every day, or we would be fat like the Americans. My siblings and I especially appreciate this food after a rough night out," he said, winking.

Then Oscar remembered their rough night. "Did you tell her about being in jail?" He started to worry that his mother may feel she was hiding a criminal.

"No, do not worry," Daniel assured him. "I did not tell her anything. They did not convict us of any crime, except my bad attitude, so there is no reason for her to know."

"Did she not ask why we did not arrive for dinner as we had planned?" Oscar asked, still trying to figure out how Daniel had explained their late arrival. "I just told her we had met some friends for dinner and went out afterwards," he explained nonchalantly.

Oscar continued, "And our backpacks? Did she not ask where we put them the whole night?"

"Mate, do NOT worry. She is a singer; she is not the type to be linear and think about proceedings in an orderly fashion," he said as if this occupation made her reactions clearer.

"A singer?" Oscar said, surprised, wondering how she could sing after smoking all of those cigarettes. The thought alone made him think of the explicit commercials he had seen showing black lungs and advising the youth to not pick up the bad habit.

"Yes, she has a brilliant voice," Daniel started singing after this comment and showed how DNA was not perfect, and in this instance his apple had fallen far from her tree.

Oscar joined in. "Every morning there's a halo hanging from the corner of my girlfriend's four post bed. I know it's not mine but I'll see if I can use it for the weekend or a one-night stand."

The singing transitioned from Sugar Ray to Back Street Boys.

"You are my fire, the one, desire. Believe, when I say…I want it that way. But we, are two worlds apart, can't reach to your heart. When you say, that I want it that way. Tell me why, ain't nothing but a heartache, tell me why, ain't nothing but a mistake. Tell me why, I never wanna hear you say, I want it that way!!!"

"I can't believe you know all the words!" Daniel said.

"I know!" Oscar said, not even knowing himself that he knew all the lyrics. "I think we heard it so many times on the train, that it got imprinted in our brains."

After they were laughing a while and had finished singing the song Daniel spoke, now a bit more serious, "You have a really good voice."

Oscar reacted, "Oh, shut up!" getting used to Daniel always making fun of him.

"I am serious!" Daniel said, actually looking like his sentiments mirrored his words.

"Ok, thanks, I guess," Oscar said, wanting to believe, but not so sure.

"I have heard so much singing because of my mother and her dragging us to concerts, operas and all that stuff. I will ask her what she thinks," Daniel said, already halfway out of the kitchen.

"No!" Oscar said louder than he expected. *"Por favor!"*

But Daniel was already on his way. He was practically dragging his mom back into the kitchen. She looked around the kitchen for an ashtray and put out her cigarette.

"Qué es? Se ha quemado algo?" she said sniffing around to see if something was burnt.

"Mama, listen to Oscar sing," Daniel said. Oscar stood there and just stared at both of them.

Daniel kept saying words of encouragement like, *"Vamos,* you can do it. Show her, you will see she says you are good."

Oscar did not feel like singing in the least.

Daniel was persistent. "Sing the Backstreet boys again. I know it is a horrible song, but your voice is clear and really melodic." It became apparent that Daniel was not going to give up.

After some more pushy words, Oscar decided that to sing something and then have the ability to leave was better than having to stand as the spectacle in the corner.

"I am not sure if you are familiar with this song." Oscar spoke slowly, unsure of Alejandra's understanding of the English language, or Portuguese for that matter.

"This is a Portuguese fado, the singer is called Amalia Rodrigues. She is very popular at home and my mom would always play her around the house. She especially liked to listen to her when she was sewing wedding gowns which seemed ironic considering most of them are very sad songs of love lost and those type of heartbreaks. One of her most famous ones that comes to mind is called *Solidao* and this song is not new; it is probably from the late 1960's." As Oscar said that, his black hair fell in his eyes and he felt like leaving it there to curtain him from the viewers.

Solidão de quem tremeu

A tentação do céu

E dos encantos, o que o céu me deu

Serei bem eu

Sob este véu de pranto

Sem saber se choro algum pecado

A tremer, imploro o céu fechado

Triste amor, o amor de alguém

The song was not long, but the silence after he finished was. Alejandra started clapping and grabbed Oscar's cheeks and kissed both of them.

"Wow, *gracias*." he said, unsure of a more wordy response to her affectionate reaction.

Daniel grinned in his "I told you so" manner. "*Te lo dije*," he nudged his mom, confirming with her what he had previously suspected.

They both shot out question after question to Oscar, who had no idea how to respond.

It was apparent to his small audience that he was not really aware of this gift they were attributing to him. They begged and pleaded, and he sang two other fado songs. He still felt embarrassed by the second one, but by the third one he was loosening up.

Clapping and more clapping followed after each song he sang and he felt very appreciated.

"*Y tu nombre es mas bien español, o se usa mucho en Portugal?* Alejandra inquired about his name origin.

Oscar explained, "It is not very common in Portugal, so people would sometimes think that I was not Portuguese, well also because of my pale skin." His skin was not so pale after the hot summer, but much lighter than everyone's, in the room.

"My mother, Odette, always loved the clothes designer Oscar de la Renta, and the fact that both her name and his name start with an O 'was a sign' she told me, so that was my name. My father, Edmundo, was not very happy with it at first, but he will never admit that. So this is my name, not much I can do about it."

"And your mother, Odette," she started to formulate a question but then changed track, "that is the name of the Swan Queen in the ballet Swan Lake. Well I am sure you were familiar with that."

"No," Oscar chose his words carefully not to offend, "actually I do not go to many ballets or operas. I usually don't even like watching musicals on television or at the cinema. I am sorry." He wanted to be apologetic but honest at the same time, afraid that if he showed a knowledge of Swan Lake, he would continue to be cornered, which was making his body radiate even more heat. If only he could slide himself into the cold refrigerator nearby and stop sweating. Daniel and Alejandra did not seem to be bothered by the heat. The sweat gave their bronzed skin and black hair a glow. Oscar pushed his own black hair off his face, and behind his ear.

Alejandra changed subjects again. "Well, I am not sure how long you are staying, but Dani, maybe you can look for a nice show to take Oscar. A flamenco where there is singing. I am sure he would love that." She nudged Daniel on the shoulder to confirm that he was listening to her, since her eyes did not leave Oscar's face.

"You know, Oscar, you and Daniel look similar. I cannot pinpoint what it is, but there is something. Definitely not the skin color, as you pointed out, but something, *algo*."

She was now speaking in her broken English, realizing that this was the language they would best understand in sync.

"Now your mama, Odette, what does she do?" she asked, hoping to know more about Oscar through his mother.

"She is a dressmaker, a seamstress, I think they call it in English." Oscar said and from Alejandra's face forward and expectant reaction, he knew she wanted more. "She specializes in wedding gowns and is very popular with the socialite women in Lisbon who search her out to design their dresses. Our living room and house are filled with beads and crystals and string and lace, and if you are lucky you won't find pins and needles on your bedroom floor."

Alejandra's face lit up when she imagined this fantastical disorder.

"See, Dani, our house is pretty tame, compared to that," Alejandra smiled satisfactorily.

Daniel did not look as convinced. "Come, Oscar, let me show you our living room."

XII

Oscar could not have been more thrilled to get out of that hot kitchen. From the size of the bathroom, kitchen and last night's bedroom, he imagined another small room, but was pleasantly surprised when they walked into a space three times the size of the kitchen, which was in a disorder, different than his house in Lisbon, but a mess just the same.

There were all types of musical instruments lying on the table, and the flute stuck inside a plant looked alienesque with green leaves coming out of it. On the floor rested a large oboe, an electric guitar, and in the corner was a harp. A striking white upright piano stood in the middle of the room. Dark wood furniture filled up every wall.

"Dad still hates that thing," he said pointing to the piano. "Well, you can imagine his face when mum brought it home."

Alejandra smiled at that with satisfaction as if she had won a bet.

"My parents are divorced and my father lives in England. We usually go visit him earlier in the summer, the only time it seems not to rain there. But even then, it usually still does." Daniel explained.

"Hola," a youngish girl said as she entered the room.

"Well, let me introduce you to my sister Laurel," Daniel said to Oscar.

"*Hola, comó te llamas?*" she said not having been given his name.

"Oscar, *mucho gusto*," he said.

Laurel asked, "Where are you from?"

Oscar explained, "I am from Portugal, Lisbon specifically. This is my first time in Spain."

Laurel smiled, "How are you liking it so far? What is your favorite part you have visited?"

He thought for a second and even though he had been away for only 48 hours, he felt he had seen a lot. "I was in Badajoz first, just for one night, and then Daniel and I met at the train station and went out and the next morning he convinced me to travel to Granada even though I was supposed to stay in that area for 3 or 4 days, or so. Yesterday we spent the day travelling by train, we went through Castilla-La Mancha region, and I think we were a little lost, or rather, took the longest possible train here, but not to worry, we have had a fine time, and I can't say which is my favorite except that I was very happy to wake up at your house in Granada this morning."

He left out the part of the jail, figuring that they would eventually know but did not need to hear about it the same moment they were introduced to him.

"*Vaya viaje*! Your English is very good," she said.

Oscar smiled, "Thank you, so is yours. I really like your British accent." Laurel smiled back.

Daniel felt a strange attraction between the two and decided to interrupt it before it went any further.

"Hey, you have never given me a compliment on my English," Daniel said, not feeling the center of attention, which was usually his default position.

"Nor you complimented mine," Oscar said, forcing a British accent and acting like he was taking off a hat and bowing in front of him.

Alejandra started telling Laurel all about Oscar's beautiful singing voice and the different fados he knew. Laurel seemed impressed and asked Oscar to sing.

Finally, Oscar thought, I am feeling comfortable and not so claustrophobic and they want me to start singing again. He regretted ever having sung; he was sure that as long as he was around Alejandra or Daniel, they would keep insisting he sing.

He was confused by all the interest in his voice. At home he would sing around the house and no one would pay attention. His mother was usually too stressed out to notice, and his father usually had his nose buried in a newspaper or book, so even if he did notice he may have thought it was the radio or just not taken much care about it.

Oscar took a deep breath and before his brain had informed his soul of the decision, his vocal chords took over and he started singing. The instruments ached to follow along but were silent without fingers to straddle them. A mix of honey and a cave, his voice warmed their spirits and they stood in silence until his last note undulated, so sad that a gentle pause was held before an eruption of applause.

Laurel's eyes sparkled, and she ran over to hug him.

"Que preciosidad! Me encanta!" she rambled on in Spanish, forgetting his limited knowledge of the language and continued to overflow him with praise as she ran again and hugged him.

Her body felt good on his, and he wrapped his arms around her. *"Gracias,"* he repeated several times. He noticed Daniel's eyes peering at him, and in that moment he did not care. Those eyes were a mixed pot of jealousy and pride melted with awe on top.

His warm face asked him for relief, and the bathroom mirror confirmed his reddened cheeks. A splash of cold water cooled him off, and he jostled with the refreshing liquid and extended it to his neck and arms. Finally, he just stuck his whole face in the filled sink, getting only half of his hair wet. That felt refreshing but incomplete, so he turned around and leaned back to get the back half portion wet as well. Grabbing the towel to dry off his dripping black locks, he looked again in the mirror and saw that it was a splashed mess so he tried drying it with the towel but instead of drops there were large streaks making the reflection blurry. He figured out that toilet paper took off the streaks and soon found out it left a thin white hair-like residue but although it was not perfect, it was the best thing he could do. He used almost half the roll to dry the floor dotted with water that had overflowed once he had sunk his whole head in the sink.

Back in the bedroom, he searched for Elena's number and sent her a text telling her he was in Granada and out of jail. He delighted in the thought of seeing her worried. Poor Elena would get a scare once she saw that.

Still feeling the high of his performance, he walked back into the music room and asked, "Besides the Alhambra, is there anything else I should see in Granada?"

"The Cathedral in Granada, most definitely," Daniel answered before anybody else was given the chance. "Isabel y Fernando los Católicos are buried in the cathedral. You want to see some dead bodies?" He raised his hands like he was a zombie, walking across the room towards Oscar.

Oscar stood there until Daniel was so close that he was going to tackle him. Oscar, despising the undead or really scary movies in general pushed him back, with more strength than he had expected and perhaps because they were the same height and weight, they both leaned backwards and fell on an instrument. Daniel's arm knocked over the violin, and its bow, like a weapon, catapulted in the air barely skimming Laurel's cheek before landing on a stack of sheet music. Oscar's body made a deafening strike against the drums and sticks, and he must have raised his hands in the wrong position because he had a harp string in his hand as he lay on the ground.

Alejandra seemed to enjoy this chaos and did not move an inch to assist any of the wounded soldiers, not that her small frame would have had the strength to pick them up.

"Look at what a symphony you are creating!" Alejandra explained. Oscar was afraid to move, embarrassed that he was holding a harp string and unsure of how exactly that had occurred.

After all the instruments were placed in their respective locations, which was easy when there was no respect to order or placement, Oscar excused himself.

XIII

Oscar closed his eyes under the cold water. What was he doing in this stranger's shower? Could somebody be showering in his bathroom in this very moment?

Had he been as easily substituted at home as he was included here in Granada?

Had Elena brought home a new boyfriend whom his parents liked better than himself, and would his place be taken over?

Were they thinking of him, as much as he was thinking of them, which was not much?

At first it would be hard for his parents if he never returned, but then they would get used to it. His mother would maybe finally have a sewing room, a place to put all of her things instead of scattering them around the dining room and living room, always complaining that she did not have enough room. It would be an organized room. A new sewing machine would be in the corner almost below the window, giving her the best light to work. The chair would also be new, comfortable with a soft pillow for her back. There would be a nice closet holding all of her threads and fabrics. The different cloths must be categorized by type and color. On the left would be the velvets and silk, on top the white, cream and light yellows, descending into blood red and black. On the right would be boxes with tiny drawers separating the needles, buttons, clasps, pins and other miniature instruments she needed to hold her ideas in place.

An antique record player would fill the room with romantic music, creating a nostalgic mood. There would be a large mirror flanked by side mirrors with a raised pedestal in front allowing a 180-degree view of Odette's creations.

The doors to the balcony would be left open in the spring to bring in more light and a slight breeze and the men and women clients would be offered a place to smoke their cigarettes outside, not intruding on the fabrics, but not limiting their habits either.

The customers would leave the room feeling renewed, their new costumes not only changing their outside appearance, but changing their lives.

Oscar stepped out of the shower and grabbed the towel, rubbing softly, then more violently. Oscar hoped to wipe away his childish longing for home and just complete the task of drying his body, rejecting his melancholic tendencies and insecurities.

There was music coming from the end of the hallway, and he picked up several instrument sounds, meaning that the Von Trapp family was busy making music. Oscar went to the bedroom and put on a clean pair of underwear.

He lay on top of the white sheets, and the deep relaxation that this induced, told him of his need for sleep. He dozed off for a while before a beeping sound woke him. Oscar reached the phone with his long arm and read a message from his sister: *Imbecil!* You better be joking. *Todo bon?*

He chuckled to himself and a good warm feeling filled his heart, making him realize that even if he was not physically present, he was still in their minds and *worry* meant love. For a second he hesitated and thought of continuing the joke to get a kick out of worrying his sister, but changed his mind and thought of his awkward moment in the shower and wanted his sister not to worry or fret over him, so he wrote back,

"Yes, it was a joke. Well, I really was in jail, but all is fine, and it was just a misunderstanding. How is everyone at home?"

He felt ridiculous for thinking of his room as a sewing area and replaced the thought with his twin bed and its dark blue bedding, chestnut desk, large rug covering up the tile floors and his bookshelf filled with collected bookends in iron, stone, carved wood and glass. His father had told him that it was good to have some type of collection, "It can be anything; as long as you see it as your own treasure, it will be a constant search in your life."

It seemed very philosophical and important when he was eight and he remembered that conversation at the beach. When they had returned home later that afternoon, his father showed him a large box with varying sizes of starfish in different shades of pink. Oscar was so excited that he dug quickly into the second box with coral and his hands started bleeding. Drops fell upon the starfish turning the pink to dark red.

"*Eu sinto papa,*" Oscar said feeling bad that he had ruined one of his father's prized starfish.

"*No, filho,* it is fine, you are excited and passionate. You will make a good collector."

From this day forward he thought of himself as a good collector: the only thing missing was the item to collect. He thought of it for weeks, then forgot about it and carried on with his regular third-grade existence. For his birthday his uncle Nuno gave him two identical hand-carved wooden horses whose tails with flowing hair seemed too big for their bodies, but Oscar did not mind. He placed them on his shelf.

The right horse was a golden brown; the wood was not treated and left in its natural form. The opposing horse was black, so dark that the facial features were indistinguishable, but it looked powerful and strong. He had asked his uncle why he had bought two horses that were the same, but different color, and Nuno admitted to Oscar that he had liked both, was too indecisive to pick a color and had purchased both hoping he would like one of them, or even better, both of them—and eventually he did.

He hugged his favorite uncle, who had also brought him a bag of *doce*, sweet and sour candy that Oscar adored. Since Oscar was little, he had always shared his birthday candy with Elena and that kept his Uncle Nuno always bringing him more, since he "respected his generosity on this ego-centric day of celebration." He had never understood what that meant, but now older, Oscar understood that his kind act had brought more kind acts, so he decided that he should continue doing what he was doing, since it was working.

The week after his 9th birthday, Oscar suddenly sat up in his bed and ran to his father in the living room.

"Papa, I have figured something out!" he pleaded and began pulling him towards his room, finally convincing him to go see what the fuss was all about.

Edmundo set his book down on the side table and followed Oscar to his room. "Look at the horses on this shelf that Uncle Nuno gave me." His father nodded and approved of his designated placement, "Yes, they look very nice there, I am glad you like both of them."

"This is it," still pointing at them, unsure why his father had not understood what he was trying to show him. "This is what I am going to collect."

"Horses?" his father asked, remembering their conversation at the beach.

"No, bookends," Oscar said. "I will collect different types: horses, other animals, soldiers, big rocks, whatever can hold my books!"

"I like it. Great idea, Son. Will I be able to put some of my books on your bookshelf, since your mother is always moving mine around or hiding them with her clothes and embellishments?"

"Of course," Oscar said, proud that his idea had been approved, and better yet, that his father wanted to participate in his collection.

"Let's put a few now!" Oscar did not want to wait, so they went around the living room and picked up books of small sizes, hardbound and others much softer with paper covers and worn edges and placed them between the horses, who held them tightly together.

XIV

Lost in his Portuguese memories, Oscar did not realize his hands were on the phone until it started ringing.

"*Estou sim? Tudo bem?*" Elena's voice was loud and hurried.

"*Si, tudo bem*, except it is hotter than hell over here," Oscar replied.

Elena said excitedly, "I don't want to hear about the weather report, I want to know if you are okay and what happened with this jail incident."

Oscar explained the arrival in the Granada train station, then backtracked and explained the night before in Badajoz, Daniel's insistence that they travel hung over to Granada that day, insisting that there was no other time to go there but that very instant.

He described the long, indirect route to get to Granada that had taken them through three regions of Spain and resulted in 12 hours of travel.

Elena was laughing and commented, "This Daniel is a particular fellow, quite eccentric it seems."

Oscar returned with, "I won't even bother telling you about Alejandra, his mother. She is another piece of work."

Suddenly, Oscar realized that although they were talking in Portuguese, Daniel and Alejandra could tune in if they heard their names mentioned in conversation.

He stopped speaking and then said, "Hold on a second."

He opened the door slightly and heard the instruments down the hallway. Returning to the bed, he propped the pillows behind his back and continued with the story.

"Well, back to the jail part," he spoke into the phone.

"Yes!! This is what I want to know about," Elena said impatiently.

"It turns out that Oscar Santos is not such a good name to have in Spain, or Granada, at least. There is a man with the same name as mine that is being sought after by the authorities."

He skipped to the end to not worry Elena. "You see my friend Daniel was able to resolve the problem. Daniel had studied law and completed his degree, but you won't believe what he decided to do instead?

"What?" Elena asked.

"To become a detective. Actually he had gotten in trouble by his university. Thinking himself the Robin Hood of the students he had taken exams from the professors and given them to the students, for a price, of course, taking from the rich students and giving to himself, the not so poor, other student. Eventually the university caught on to what was going on, once all the students were getting such high scores. He was never convicted of anything, but they hoped he would never practice law and their wishes came true since he decided to focus on detective work. Apart from that he is a actually very smart—mischievous yes, but with a good heart, I think."

"That, *I think* bothers me, but we will talk more about this Daniel later. I want to know what this other Oscar Santos is accused of?" Elena asked.

Oscar now wished he had not given away so much information, so he got back on track of the story.

"Actually, for a terrorist attempt. It was not clear if he had done any terrorist acts or was just associated with people in a terrorist organization. Whatever the details, it seems that this is not a good guy."

Elena wanted more details, "Which terrorist organization is it?"

"The Basques: they are a separatist group in the north of Spain, at the other extreme of the country, not sure why they would be trying to bomb people down here, but I guess it is as good as any other place. Daniel explained that they are a very violent group, wanting separation from Spain. They want to be their own country and call their territory, the País Vasco."

Oscar continued, "Their language, Euskera, it is called, is some ancient derivative of they don't know what. Seriously, they have not been able to figure out where it came from since it does not share any roots with the Latin languages like ours.

"Maybe I should go up there to do some archeological research. Perhaps I will turn up some old manuscripts and be able to decipher their origins." He said this with a different accent to appear older and wiser.

"Oh great, here we go with your Indiana Jones dreams of discovering treasures. Well if you do, you better name one in my honor."

They laughed. "Yes, I will call the first cave I discover: the Elena cave. As for the first ancient corpse I unearth, if it is female, she will have your name."

More laughing through the devices, and Elena responded, "No! I don't want a dead body named after me!"

Before Oscar could respond, an operator informed them that there was only one minute left on Elena's calling card.

"I will fill up my card soon. Now you stay out of trouble!" Elena said quickly signaling the end of their conversation.

"Yes, I will recharge my phone; it may have taken some minutes off my card too. Do you know how that works, with the roaming and all?" he asked.

"No I am not sure, maybe ask Daniel, he seems to have travelled a lot."

"Good idea, *sorella*. I will. *Beisos* for mama and papa, and you."

"Of course and–" Before she could continue, the conversation had ended.

Oscar walked with a different energy down the hall, knowing that even if he wasn't in Lisbon his soul was slightly there and he was not forgotten. His sister always had good timing, and he felt thankful for her and realized that his parents had created a strong bond between them. His mother always said, "Love and respect your sister. There is nobody in the world that you will know longer in your lifetime."

He also felt so appreciative for his Uncle Nuno, who had left a generous amount of money to Elena and him. Without it, his travels would not have been possible, and the gratitude was mixed with regret. Nuno's motorcyle accident had been so sudden and unexpected. He died quickly, before they could reach the hospital and Oscar had never been able to say goodbye. Oscar's eyes gazed through the window. He wondered what he would have said to him if he knew it would have been a last goodbye. Oscar formed an x with his arms in front of himself and beat his fists on his chest. Nuno had done this when he said goodbye; it was his way of expressing love for his family.

XV

In the music room, glasses were brimming with cold orange Fanta, and the sugar brought energy to the hot day. There were fans whizzing around on both sides of the room. They served as a noisy distraction, failing to lower the temperatures and simply transferring the hot air from the wall edges into the center of the room.

"My mom just reminded me that the Alhambra is open tonight really late," Daniel said. "I had completely forgotten about it. About twice a year, they open it late into the evening as a special event and, lucky for us, it is tonight."

"Great," Oscar said, not sure of what the luck was about until Daniel explained.

"You see, it is so hot during the day and many of the gardens are directly in the sun, so at night it is much cooler and you can see everything lit up. I have only seen it that way once, and always said that we should do it another time, but you know how it is. When you live somewhere, there will always be another time to do it. With you here, you create an immediacy."

Daniel continued, "Many of the rooms that are now covered used to have no roofs, but after the Reconquista, coverings were added and some modifications were made. Well, I will bring one of my guidebooks to give you all the details of the history, dates and all that. Let's plan on going around 6pm. If you do not mind, I would like to nap a little before going. You know, us Spaniards love our *siesta*." Daniel smiled, taking the best of the Spaniards and Brits and appropriating the customs as he pleased.

As Oscar pondered whether to take a nap, a small dog ran towards him and jumped on his lap, almost knocking down his melting drink. The black and white dog looked to be a Boston terrier mix, not very large but with solid muscles.

"Who is this?" he inquired.

Alejandra made the introduction. "Mussolini."

The others stared at Oscar to see his reaction. Oscar simply grabbed the dog's paw and said, *"Muito gusto,* Mussolini."

Laurel said, "You can call him Mussi for short if Mussolini seems too serious. This name was my mom's idea, as you can imagine." She looked towards her mom, rolling her eyes.

"You want to take him out for a walk?" Daniel asked, raising his arms with a big yawn in his mouth.

This actually seemed like a good idea to Oscar, and he agreed.

"There is a small park down the way and Mussi just loves to play there," Daniel said, handing Oscar the dog leash.

The idea of leaving the hot apartment was appealing. Oscar attached the leash to the dog's silver collar, walked down the stone stairs, and exited through the creaky wooden door. The cobblestone streets were bright with the Mediterranean sun.

After just a few minutes of walking, Oscar heard his name being called. He turned around and saw Alejandra waving her hands at him. He wondered what she wanted. Perhaps to send him to do an errand?

"Let's walk *juntos,*" she paused. "Together," she said the last word slowly as she intertwined her arm with his.

This is strange, thought Oscar. They continued to walk for another block in silence. Oscar could not think of what to say, but he felt that she had a lot to say. When she finally started speaking, she mentioned the weather.

"*Que calor!*" were Alejandra's first words.

"Yes," Oscar said afraid of appearing rude by letting go of her sticky arm that was now melted into his being. She must have read his mind as she let go shortly after and hunched down towards Mussi. She moved in slow motion, patting the dog's hair over and over. Under a shady tree, they passed the time in silence and when Alejandra stood up they started walking.

"You must be curious about Lawrence?" Alejandra said looking ahead in the distance.

"I'm sorry. Who is that?"

"Daniel's father. Has he not spoken about him?"

"Yes, but I guess he never mentioned his name."

"I see."

They passed a kiosk selling flowers, as two men tried tying a bouquet of roses to the rack above the back tire.

"Is he still alive?" Oscar wondered.

"Oh yes. He lives in England, but only some of the children speak to him. It is *complicado.*" Alejandra cleared her throat. "Your mother travelled to England a while back. Isn't that right?"

Oscar tried to figure out what year it had been, but between the lack of sleep and sudden feeling of dehydration, he could not remember.

"How old are you, Oscar?"

"Twenty-five."

"Is it possible that your mom went to England in 1972?"

"Sure, I mean, it was before I was born so maybe a year or two before that. I am not sure. Why do you ask?"

Alejandra stopped at a bench and settled there. "I am not really sure how to say this." She patted the seat next to her and Oscar sat reluctantly, as far as was politely possible.

"What is it?" Oscar looked ahead, as did she.

"Your mother and Lawrence met in England that summer she was visiting. They fell in love, sort of, well, *no se*. They met and fancied each other."

"How do you know this?" Oscar asked.

"I found their correspondence, not at the time, just a few years ago. After we divorced. We were married when this occurred, but that is not of importance now."

"I don't understand. Why are you telling me this?"

"This is not easy to say, Oscar. We barely know each other, but it is important. I would want to know if a secret like this had been kept from me."

"Why should I care if they met?"

"Oscar, your mother got pregnant that summer. Lawrence is your father."

Oscar stood up and crossed his arms tightly against his body. Alejandra leaned over, with her hands over her mouth.

"I think you must be mistaken. My father's name is Edmundo."

"I'm sorry, I really am. I should not be the one telling you this. I am sure he is a *gran persona*," she paused. "I wasn't expecting this conversation to be easy. It couldn't be, no matter how you describe it. I may not be making much sense now. But, it is okay, it is normal to be shocked. I am sorry, I don't know how to comfort you."

Oscar turned away from her. He stood very still looking out at the bleached white buildings. The passerby's stained the walls with their shadows and moved onward.

Oscar felt unable to breathe, much less move. He closed his eyes and listened to the carousel's repeating music that played behind the walls.

He finally spoke, "Alejandra, I think there has been a mistake. No, I am sure of it. I don't know this person named Lawrence, and I am sure that my father is Edmundo. My parents are happily married and my mother would not..." Oscar searched for better words. "This is not my story, it is somebody else's. You are mistaken."

"I don't expect you to believe me. I did not make this up. Daniel can show you."

"Daniel knows about this?"

"Yes, he has all the letters."

"Wait a second, Daniel believes this story too? Does he think we are...brothers? I mean, wait a second...did he find me through his detective work?"

"Daniel can tell you how he found you, but yes. Daniel knows the truth and wanted to share it with you. He thought it would be best if I told you. He just doesn't know I was going to do it right now."

Alejandra had tears in her eyes. "I am sorry, again, *perdoname*, but I could not wait any longer. We have wanted to meet you for a long time, and I was afraid that you might disappear tomorrow and the chance would be gone. Daniel will understand my haste."

"What do you mean a long time? How long? Honestly, I don't even care. This conversation is over."

"Wait." Alejandra put her arms around him.

Oscar walked quickly through the steamy streets and reached a bridge. He stopped and did not like the feeling of being still, so he continued until his mouth was as salty as the sea and his shirt was stuck to his skin.

He found a bar and ordered a Coca Cola, finished it and then ordered a bottle of sparkling water.

It's not known how much time passed, but pass it did, and Oscar began to wonder how he had never asked himself any of these questions. How was it possible to look in the mirror and not see?

"It can't be," he said out loud. They must have mistaken him for somebody else, just like the occurrence at the train station. There must be another Oscar Santos and this trip was one confusing mess of identities. Daniel's detective skills were probably not as sharp as he envisioned them.

He had to speak to Daniel, to figure out where the mistake was. They should be looking for the other Oscar: the one with the missing father. He didn't have a missing father. He knew exactly where he was born, who his parents were. He had one sister named Elena and a very stable, if sometimes, predictable life, but that was it. There was no other father or family, and why was he even in Granada?

Why had he followed Daniel so eagerly? Sure, Daniel was very persistent, but the whole short time felt speeded up and slowed down at the wrong times. They had been rushing from one place to another and for what reason?

Maybe Daniel was simply crazy and had made up this whole story. These postcards were probably Daniel's way to get attention in a family with many children. Perhaps Daniel was a compulsive liar and did this all the time?

It was not too late. Nothing was keeping him in Granada. He would simply get his bags and money and leave. Oh no, what a novice! Perhaps Daniel was trying to rob him and this was all a setup.

Oscar felt dizzy. He looked around and wasn't sure where he was in the city. He rapidly asked the waiter, got directions, paid his bill and headed towards Daniel's house.

The streets were a maze. After an hour he felt he was close but started panicking that he would never find the house. His passport, his money and all of his belongings were at a house he could not find. And the people in it, he barely knew. He had been too trusting, a child. How would he explain this when he got home?

That was it. Call Elena. But...what could she do? She would worry and tell his parents.

Oscar thought of his father. The father he loved but had never completely connected with... His heart hurt. He pushed the lies out of his head. His body was shaking, and he pressed his hand to his heart. More shaking. Finally, he realized it was his phone. He looked down and saw a missed call from Monica.

XVI

Oscar just stared at Monica's name on his phone and took a deep breath. A few seconds later, a message beeped in:

"I am walking around close to the Cathedral. What are you doing *Portugues*?"

He was happy to hear from her. He liked her, and it was stupid to let this fantastical story bother him. He knew who he was. Son of Odette and Edmundo, and Alejandra's made-up fable was not going to bother him. Did he even want to go back to Daniel's? Yes, he was not afraid. He would tell him about his conversation with Alejandra, and they would have a laugh at the absurdity of it all. Perhaps Lawrence had met a woman named Odette. That could be true. But it wasn't his mother, and Lawrence was not his father. How easily he had fallen trap into the hands of a mad woman. There was no rush to get back—enjoy the moment. He was having a grand time. Adventure was what he wanted, and that was exactly what he was going to get.

Meeting Monica sounded like the perfect thing to do. He could later decide if he wanted to tell her of this crazy story.

"Just strolling around the city. Getting a little lost. :-) Want to grab a drink?"

"Sure, let's meet by the cathedral. We can check it out first *y despues tomar una cerveza*."

"*Claro que sí*. See you shortly."

He asked for directions and realized he was not too far away from Monica's location. Within ten minutes he arrived and saw her, more beautiful than ever. In that moment he forgot about Alejandra, and her ridiculous theories.

Monica was studying a large map of sorts. Her long black hair was pulled back in a ponytail and rested on her left shoulder. She was wearing a white skirt that touched right above her knees and a black sleeveless top with crochet designs along her back. Her feet were covered with white and black polka dots, and long laces spiraled up her tan legs and ended in bows beneath her knees.

"*Hola española*," Oscar said loudly.

"*Hola!*" her smile could be felt across the cobblestones. She pointed towards the floor. "Why are you holding a dog?"

Oscar looked down at Mussi, who was now at Monica's feet trying to climb up her legs.

"Ha, I had forgot about him. He is Daniel's dog. Alejandra and I went for a walk and she left and I got stuck walking him around. He is quite friendly, I really don't mind."

"Who is Alejandra?" Monica asked opening up her already big eyes.

"Oh! Sorry, she is Daniel's mom."

"Huh, that is interesting. Did you know Daniel and his family before you met him on this trip?"

That question caught Oscar off guard. "No, not at all. It was a chance meeting."

Wait a minute, Oscar thought. Perhaps it was not by chance. Maybe Daniel followed him to Extremadura. But how could he know he would be there? It had to be a coincidence. The more Oscar thought about it, the more he thought that it was, instead, precisely intentional. Daniel had moved them from one place to another quickly and irrationally to get them to Granada. But why? So he could talk to Alejandra, so they could tell him their outlandish theory? It was just one big misunderstanding. Perhaps, Alejandra had told him this story so he would leave. No, that was the stupidest thing he could think. She kept insisting that he stay as long as possible. She had hugged him for longer than normal when they said goodbye. He never hugged anybody like that after knowing them for such a short time.

"Are you okay?" Monica said.

Oscar didn't realize he had been staring out towards the large glass window across the way.

"*Sí, perdón.*" He forced a smile and neared closer to her to avoid looking in her eyes.

Oscar moved to give her a kiss on the cheek but instead planted a kiss on her lips, pressing hard and surprising her and himself.

"Oscar! Good to see you too!" She started laughing, so he kissed her again, putting his arms around her waist and bringing her closer to him.

She closed her eyes while she kissed him, and it was something that he liked. He didn't know why.

"I just want to live in a world where chickens could cross the street and not be asked what their intentions are," Oscar said.

Monica started laughing, and then Oscar followed and within minutes they were in tears, not knowing why they were laughing.

"Why would you say that?" Monica asked.

"Honestly, I am not sure. I saw that on a windowpane as I was walking over here and I could not get it out of my head. I just thought it was funny in an odd way."

"My parents have a bunch of plaques in their kitchen with different sayings. Do you remember where the shop is?"

"I think it was that way." He pointed towards the street lined with overgrown trees spilling over a black iron fence.

"Okay, let's go after we visit the Cathedral. Wait! I am not really sure if we could go in now? What will we do with Mussi?"

Mussi jumped up when he heard his name and ended up in Monica's arms.

"Mussolini, *venha aqui*! I don't want him to dirty your white skirt," Oscar said, reaching out for the dog.

"I don't mind. I love dogs. I can wash it later, and maybe I will meet a nice *Portugues* boy at the Laundromat. I didn't know that was such a hotspot to meet people," Monica said with a wink.

"It definitely is. I have used it on the odd Saturday when there is nothing to do in Lisbon and I wanted to escape my family. I would walk down to the Laundromat and there were plenty of hot girls removing their clothes and throwing them into the washer. It was like a visit to the Red District in Amsterdam!" Oscar said with a smile. Monica smiled and shook her head. " I doubt that!"

The dog jumped out of Monica's arms and onto to the cobblestones. It sat and looked up at her attentively. Monica kneeled down and shook his paw.

"Mussolini! What kind of a dog name is that? They might as well have kept it more nationalistic and named you Francisco Franco!" she said, and they both laughed.

"*Franco, Franco, tiene el culo blanco y su mujer también, lo lavan con Ariel*." Oscar sang.

Monica's mouth opened. "How do you know that song?"

Oscar recounted the story that Daniel had told him, and they both pictured Daniel as a small child and all his siblings marching around the beach apartment in unison.

"Where is Daniel?" Monica asked.

"At home taking a siesta. How very Spanish."

"Where about does he live?"

"*En el Albaicín*," Oscar was surprised he remembered the area.

"*En el Albaicín?*" she asked in a surprised tone.

"Yes, why do you say it that way?" he asked, wondering if he had pronounced it wrong.

"It's just that this is the area where all the *gitanos* live, and I am surprised he would live there," she said and immediately looked like she regretted her words.

"I will make sure not to get robbed when I walk back. Even though, I have been to two of the jails," he said in a flat voice.

"What! What happened? When?" she raised her hands questioningly.

Oscar enjoyed seeing her excited. He found her so beautiful, passionate, and especially liked it when she was surprised like this.

He described in full detail their adventure the night before, and his description led to more questions from Monica, so Oscar embellished certain parts to make it more interesting.

The church bells started ringing loudly.

"Is this the Cathedral of Granada?" Oscar asked.

"Yes, it is open for another hour if you want to go," she said looking at her watch.

They started walking towards it, and Monica pointed to the dog. "What are you going to do with Mussi?"

"I have an idea," Oscar said.

Monica wondered what he was planning to do, so Oscar explained to her his idea and when they arrived at the entrance, Monica played her part.

"*Esta segura?*" the old lady behind the counter asked as Monica explained that the tiny black and white dog was a seeing eye dog. Oscar attempted a blank expression in his stare and looked everywhere except the direction of the voices, avoiding eye contact.

The white-haired lady asked to speak to Oscar and when he spoke to her, he crouched down to the window. He spoke quickly in a Portuguese dialect. He explained to her that he was blind, and needed a seeing eye dog at all times.

She didn't understand his words, but realized that he was saying he was blind. She glanced at the clock and with her hand indicated they could go.

Monica spoke to a motionless Oscar and explained that they were allowed to enter, grabbed his arm and led him to the entrance. At that same time the old lady muttered under her breath, "Why does he even want to go in, if he can't see anything?"

They toured the cathedral arm and arm with Mussolini still smelling everything but not finding any dog scents he liked. He was not convincing as a seeing-eye dog. The children who were with their parents inside of the cathedral ran to him, and he jumped into the arms of anybody who would pet him.

Oscar got better and better at playing the part and Monica explained to him the history of the cathedral and they finally saw the resting place of the *Reyes Católicos*, as Isabel and Ferdinand were referred to in Spain. The Catholic Kings was the translation, as if the other royalty had not been Catholic enough.

Oscar and Monica debated who had been the best explorers and Oscar's version of the Portuguese discoveries was much different than what Monica had learned in school, making apparent that history books were written by the winners. Their countries seemed to have modified the retelling of events.

Oscar suddenly looked down at his watch, seeing that he did not have one on and forgetting for an instant that he was supposed to act blind.

"What time is it?" Oscar asked.

Monica checked her watch and saw that it was nearing six o'clock. Once she informed Oscar, he said that he better hurry back. They proceeded toward the exit, which was in the same place as the entrance, and because he couldn't help himself, Oscar bowed with his head to the old lady and looked her straight in the eyes. At first look, she did not react, but her eyes widened as she realized that Oscar had been faking it, and he smirked, and Monica could not hold her laughter as they pulled Mussolini out of the cathedral and out into the streets.

Oscar was relieved that there was little time to spare before their next activity. Perhaps he would speak to Daniel after he had a few drinks. He climbed the stairs with some apprehension.

"Good timing, I was afraid you had forgotten," Daniel said, opening the door.

Oscar looked into his eyes. He inspected his nose and mouth, the shape of his ears, the length of his arms. He could not take his eyes off of their mirrored heights and body build.

"What's up? *Me miras tan raro,*" Daniel said with a confused face.

"Sorry, I was just thinking of Monica and I don't want to be late. You know I just ran into her and we hung out at the Cathedral."

"Sexy place to hang," Daniel smirked.

"I'm going to shower quickly and then we can go," Oscar said and headed down the hall.

After checking his belongings, Oscar let out a sigh of relief and ended up hiding his passport and money in the first place that came to mind. Why did people always hide valuables under a mattress? If he were a thief, he would look there first. Humans are creatures of habit.

Many thoughts entered Oscar's mind during his brief shower. When should he speak to Daniel? Should Alejandra be there? He wanted to inspect the postcards, but how could he really tell if they were authentic? Even better question, WHY would anybody want to make up a story of this caliber?

XVII

Monica was waiting at the entrance when they arrived to the Alhambra. Because Daniel was a local, he flashed his identification card and was not asked to pay the entrance fee. Oscar paid 500 pesetas, a discounted ticket since he was a member of the European Union. Monica spoke to the ticket officer and, even though she had forgot her i.d., they could tell from her accent that she was a local; her voice and pretty smile convinced the officer, and they entered the first room through a half-moon archway.

Three similar archways led in and out of this room. It was open to the sky and the map called it an atrium. There was a striped brick pattern across the walls and Roman bases supported the columns.

Oscar noted to Monica that had the columns been connected with the floor without the base, it would have been in the Greek style.

Monica commented, "I love learning anything new about the Alhambra. Did you study art in college? You know, I have been speaking so much about myself, but you never told me what you do."

Oscar was pleased that she was taking an interest, since he could tell that Daniel was yearning for her attention.

"Actually, I just finished my degree in anthropology, with an emphasis in archeology. I ended up taking several art history courses required by my degree, and continued with a few more in ancient Greek and Roman history for my extra credit since it really fascinated me."

Again, Monica seemed pleased and followed Oscar into the next area.

Daniel felt that he had to chime in with his two cents. With the guidebook in hand, he read aloud, stressing his British accent. "The Alhambra was built between 1338 to 1390, and you will never guess this, but there is no known architect attributed to this building. In several rooms we will be in the Patio de los Arrayanes which is known as one of the best uses of the unique geometric pattern, established in this period."

Daniel was having fun with this and continued to read the description from the pamphlet they were given which featured a large map of the entire area. "This sprawling complex is comprised of the royal residential quarters, and the servant's buildings flanked by official chambers, baths and a mosque for praying. The entire building gave hints and indications of rooms for meditation and reflection. The Lion Court is the most famous of the rooms, so we must definitely see that. Supposedly, it is the Islamic version of paradise made into a physical room. Not sure what the lions have to do with Paradise, but we will see it shortly. It is towards the beginning," he said as he pointed to the next area following the entrance.

Monica did not pay as much attention to him and flanked Oscar's side in the Court of the Myrtles. They stood in awe at the beautiful outdoor pool. It was shallow, so it would not have been used for swimming. The bottom was not totally apparent but it was definitely not deep enough for a human body. They all guessed at its use, and Oscar asked for Daniel's guidebook.

With the guidebook in Oscar's hand, Daniel felt he was no longer needed.

The next room was a marvel almost indescribable. The archways were similar to those in the first room, but in the middle there was a large squared pool that held the perfect reflection of these archways in the water. A large squared tower was behind it with small windows possibly where guns could have hidden to surprise intruders, in other words, the Spanish who were trying to reclaim their land, which the Moors were reclaiming in the first place.

Every room flowed into the next, each with its unique nature but sharing the Moorish design of keyhole windows, more arches, more water and more geometric patterns.

The last interior room had all four walls decorated in ornamental reliefs made of stone, and Oscar got close up to inspect the gold and azure miniature mosaics. He could tell they had been hand cut and tried to imagine the hours spent planning out just this single wall. The mosaic design followed the pathway to the next rooms, which showed central flowers within squares decorated on each corner with blue and yellow birds, holding either a small worm or leaf in their beaks.

Following a long pathway, a keyhole-shaped large archway gave a direct view to a path that was lined with flowers on both sides and at its finish a decorative palace with tall cypress trees peeking out of its rooftops. They ventured through the Generalife and viewed the outside gardens, patios filled with orange and lemon trees, bougainvillea bushes sprouting with bright fuchsia colors, decorating the iron doors and making it sometimes difficult to close them.

The sun was starting to lower from their sight and head on its path to illuminate another part of the world.

"I read about Bill Clinton's visit here last year," Oscar explained. "He had originally visited the Alhambra 30 years earlier and remembered it as the place with the most beautiful sunset. Last year he brought Hillary and his daughter to see the sunset again, and he said it was just as impressive."

Oscar grabbed Monica's hand. "Come, I will show you."

XVIII

As they walked towards the desired spot, Daniel was nowhere in sight. The water trickled down the stairs and the sweet flower smell relaxed them on their walk. Openings through the barrier walls gave way to immense views of the city.

"Look at the sun hiding behind that mountain," Oscar said as he pointed to the distance and could cover the sun with one finger and one eye closed.

"If you stand really still and close your eyes, you can actually feel the earth move away from the sun," Monica said and closed her eyes when she finished the sentence, making sure she was speaking the truth.

In that moment, Oscar leaned down and inched his head down from the height of the trees, towards her face, placing a kiss on her lips.

When he leaned back, she opened her eyes and tiptoed to his height to return the gift. Oscar took her in his arms and as they turned towards the sun, they saw it was no longer there. An orange, yellow and pink light floated in the sky, but it was faint and disappearing slowly.

The night had brought cooler temperatures, but their bodies were hot with attraction to the setting and to each other. Oscar had usually thought it through much more before kissing a girl, but in this maze of fountains and rooms, he had felt suspended in a different time, making him a different person.

Could it be that he was in a different country? Was that what was making him different? He discarded these thoughts and held Monica a little tighter, finally letting go when he saw that their arms were beading up with moisture from the proximity of their skin.

When he separated, it made a sucking sound, and it made them smile, creating complicity between them and although it would have been possible and likely to feel uncomfortable after this unexpected moment, they felt at ease in their own skin and with each other's company.

"Boabdil, o Boabdil el Chico was the name of the son of the Sultans who lost the kingdom of Granada. Have you heard of the famous saying that his mother told him?" Monica asked.

Oscar laughed because he thought of all the sayings he had learned in just three days of being in Spain.

"Do you know it?" Monica assuming his laughter meant he found it comical.

"No, please tell me. It's just that you Spaniards have tons of sayings. I like it, actually."

"*Vale.* So Boabdil's mother was called Sultana Aixa, well, probably Aixa or rather just Mama to him. You actually pronounce it *mama* in Arabic, *como en español.* Aixa and her son Boabdil left Granada and were hiding in the Alpujarras mountains. Boabdil was crying and his mother said to him, "*Llora como mujer lo que no supiste defender como hombre.*"

"*Llora* is that cry in Spanish?" Oscar asked.

"Yes, she told her son, 'Cry like a woman for that which you have not been able to defend like a man,'" Monica translated.

"Wow, that is powerful," Oscar said.

"It has never been officially documented that she said that, but it is a legend repeated for many years. The mountain where this was supposedly said has been named el *Suspiro del Moro.*"

"Will you take me there?" Oscar said, touching the side of her face.

117

"Yes, it is worth a trip. The Alpujarras are probably cooler than the city."

Oscar realized that he and Monica had completely forgotten about Daniel, and Daniel in turn had tried to forget about them.

Daniel looked around to see if there were any interesting women in his vicinity, careful to not have them see him eyeing them. He rarely approached girls and found it easier when they came into his territory. Having watched his brother's pathetic attempts to get women, he found a strategy of his own and his philosophy was "the nicer you are, the less they will want to give you." He figured that humans were not that complicated- in reverse the strategy was successful. The less he gave them, the nicer the women were, and this led them to get anxious, feel they were owed upon and in return, wait around for a pay back. So when he went to bars, he never paid for their drinks. Instead, they paid for his.

Two Swedish girls were looking at him between the trees and whispering to each other. Daniel continued reading his book, intermittently looking up to view the architecture he was studying. Yes, he was a good-looking guy, much taller than the other Spaniards, and this was evident even if he was sitting down.

The taller of the two approached him, asking about one of the buildings, pointing to the small map in her hand. He looked up from his book and smiled in a way that made his eyes squint and sparkle.

He repeated the name and, checking his guidebook, he found the building in question and, with most beautiful Spanish, explained its location and some facts about its origin. The two blondes looked at each other and tried responding back in Spanish.

Daniel leaned in close and said in a very proper accent, "Do you speak English?"

They seemed relieved that they did speak a shared language, so they engaged in a simple conversation.

"I'm Daniel."

"Anna," said the taller blonde, extending her hand to shake his.

"Actually, that is considered very Northern here. In Spain, we greet each other with two kisses. If you don't mind," Daniel said with a smile. Anna smiled back. Daniel leaned in and kissed both her cheeks.

"Mucho gusto," Daniel said and she repeated his words.

"Hi, I'm Kim," said the other Swede and leaned in to receive Daniel's kisses.

Anna and Kim described their summer travels and mentioned that they were nearing the end of their holiday. They spoke of the art they had seen at the Guggenheim museum in Bilbao and Dali's museum on the Costa Brava near Barcelona.

"*Figueras*," Daniel said slowly and the Swedes repeated. It seemed like a tongue twister to them and they were dizzy with Daniel's charm and the difficulty of pronouncing this word.

Oscar eyed Daniel speaking to the whitish blonde-haired girls and gave him some space, so he could continue his flirting.

XIX

It was nearing 10pm in the evening. Oscar and Monica approached Daniel holding hands.

"Tonight nobody sleeps. *Copas, tapas y discoteca*," Daniel said enthusiastically.

The Swedes had gone home to drop off their tourist trinkets and had promised to meet Daniel at the bar at 10pm.

"They will probably be here soon. The Swedes are Northern Europeans and they are never late."

"Maybe they won't come. You might have scared them with your expansive knowledge of the Alhambra," Oscar said sarcastically.

"Please! Women love me, especially the blondes swoon over my dark-haired good looks," Daniel smirked.

Monica chimed in, "Well, they might end up liking Oscar too." She did a double take between them, "You guys actually look alike, are you cousins?"

Daniel and Oscar stared at each other without noticing that their mouths were slightly in awe. Oscar did not say anything, waiting to see Daniel's reaction.

"It may appear so, but I am much better looking." Daniel tried smiling, but his comment came out flat.

An awkward silence followed and Monica broke it, "I guess you are right, about the Northern Europeans, that is," pointing to the Swedish girls walking down the street. "But I think Oscar is better looking!" and sje planted a kiss on his cheek.

Oscar returned the kiss on Monica's cheek and drew her closer to him, softly kissing her on the top of her head. It seemed almost too affectionate of a gesture, something for a small child, but he felt full of love for her, that she had chosen him. He felt a bigger distance from Daniel than he expected. He didn't need him; they were just new-found friends, nothing more than that.

The dinner was spent standing around a large wooden barrel. It was turned upside down, no longer holding wine, but rather empty plates littered with used toothpicks.
The bar worked on an honor system. A long counter in front of the bartenders displayed small and large plates with toothpicks pointing out of each item. At the end of the evening, the server would count the toothpicks and charge the customers accordingly.

The fish selection was *pulpo en su tinta, boquerones en vinagre, sepia frita,* and small toasted pieces of bread with fried fish and parsley on top. The vegetarian options were *pimientos rojos* and *zarangollo,* a mix that is sautéed and baked for a long time made up of zucchini, onions, garlic, leeks and carrots. The most varied choices were for the carnivores; every type of cold cut was laid out in an artistic formation. Slices of salami were rolled up with mango and mint. Jamón was laid out on the crusty bread drenched in truffle oil. Another plate had pieces of thin steak with foie grois and a sliver of lemon.

With each trip to the counter, the bartender took their drink orders, which consisted of Cerveza San Miguel for the men, and sangria for the girls. The bottles of Lanjarón were everywhere, celebrating the local water.

They drank and ate and feasted some more, indulging in fresh raspberry cream cakes topped with lemon sorbetto.

121

Daniel led the group to a music bar by the river. There was music blasting and drinks flowing, and they sang to the old Bon Jovi hit:

"Oh, we are half way there! Oh, oh, living on a prayer, take my hand and I'll make it, I swear.. Oh, oh, living on a prayer."

The one-hit wonder by Europe, "Final Countdown" followed: *"It's the Final Countdown, na na na na…"*

Nobody knew the words very well, but they laughed and cheered as the drinks alleviated their thirst and welcomed the darkness of the night.

Following the river, they found a carnival in full swing. The Ferris wheel sparkled with green and yellow lights, and the bumper cars called their name. The five of them stepped into different cars and bumped each other until Monica almost fell out of hers. Daniel was the culprit. He would get really close behind Monica, and thumped her car with all his strength.

Oscar followed Daniel and pushed him into a corner. The Swedes were having difficulty backing up their car and continued riding around in reverse, causing a traffic jam.

"Vamos a hacer un botellón," Daniel exclaimed. Monica was the only one who knew what that meant. They went to a brightly lit store, bought a bottle of vodka, Fanta Limón and several large plastic cups. They strolled by the river where only a small stream of water meandered below, a remnant of the murderous drought.

Across the way, a large children's playground called to them, dotted with metal swings, bouncing horses and a rock-climbing wall. Thick spongy rubber covered the ground and they created a cocktail area using the equipment as side tables for their drinks. A wide tunnel was adjacent to the playground.

Music filled the air as other young people engaged in their own *botellones* on the other side of the river. This was the Spaniard witching hour when conversation was drowned out by song.

Monica and Oscar separated from the group and went on a walk. Daniel was playing bartender with the Swedes and when he turned to the side he found one of them kissing him. He saw Anna, the shyer one sitting across the way and watching them. He half stood up and grabbed her hand towards them, he was confident that she was feeling the energy by the look of her pale blue eyes. He leaned in to kiss her as he held Kim's waist.

The love triangle continued and hands travelled in ecstasy through the darkness of the night, and their distance from the lights made their play private to the others.

Anna and Kim lay on the black rubber with Daniel between them, sweat on all of their bodies and shirts misbuttoned and hair everywhere but in its place. They were all giggling, surprised by what had just occurred, and Daniel made drinks to alleviate their thirst.

"No vodka, just Fanta," Anna said.

Oscar and Monica returned with lips swollen and sensed immediately that sex was in the air. They made fresh drinks and, like children, started playing on the swings. The sweet Fanta spilled down their arms.

Daniel descended the aluminum slide with trouble, his hips too wide for a span meant to hold young children. With great effort, the Swedes attempted to teeter-totter.

Through the tunnel there was a life-size game of chess. The group decided to play a game—girls vs. boys. The girls set up the white pieces, and Oscar nudged Daniel when the girls were no longer able to hear them.

"So what happened? Your hair is really messed up." Oscar pointed.

Daniel laughed as he adjusted his hair back. "You know, those Scandinavian girls are not like our Mediterranean women." He winked at him and gave a gentleman's smile without further explanation.

Oscar put the rook in the corner and kicked Daniel when he knocked down their black king. "Don't screw us up, before we start. It's bad luck to drop the king before you start." Oscar attempted to knock Daniel over and the boys wrestled for a while before Oscar was able to pin him down, Daniel more tired than Oscar from the energy exuded.

"Winner!" Oscar exclaimed as he raised his arms in a victory chant jumping up and down above the chess pieces.

Oscar finished placing their pieces in order, the rooks on both corners. Next were the knights, one on each side, then the bishops, the king and the queen on her color square, which on their side was black. In front of these pieces the eight shorter pawns stood erect, protecting the figures behind them.

The girls were white so they began the game, placing one of the middle pawns two places forward. Daniel jumped forward and placed their pawn directly in front of theirs, avoiding any forward movement by that piece. Kim placed another pawn forward, diagonally protecting the initial pawn. Oscar felt it was his turn to decide, so he took out the knight and basically had to push it back and take it around to get it to its position or else he may have risked knocking down any of the pawns, and he was very superstitious about knocking down any of the pieces.

Monica took out her queen diagonally threatening the knight, but Daniel checked and it was protected.

However, her taking the queen out so early in the game made the young men feel that they were playing offensive.

Oscar and Daniel spoke between each other and decided to also move their queen forward two spaces. In order to put pressure in the center of the game, Anna move the knight forward diagonal from the center pawn, threatening the black pawn that was doubly protected by the knight and the queen.

Oscar moved the black pawn in front of the queen one move forward. The girls continued playing an aggressive game and moved the knight forward to threaten the queen. Upon doing that, they realized that the pawn move had served a purpose, which was to let the bishop protect the queen, although it was already protected by the pawn.

The girls did not mind losing the knight for a queen, since it was usually very difficult to win a game with a lost queen. Instead the boys surprised them and checked their king. The girls started yelling and moving around quickly, trying to see the pieces in a better way and figure out what to do.

The game continued with hunger and destruction. The boys made a foolish mistake, and in the end were forced to surrender.

XX

Oscar awoke and prepared his belongings for their trip to the sea. When he saw his beach towel, he instantly felt uncertain. Should he take it there and then have the same towel as Monica and look ridiculous? He could attribute the towel to a coincidence. On the other hand, he also wanted to tell her about this story, maybe it would create a connection with her, or would she find him creepy or obsessive? She had kissed him, so she must not find him that appalling.

Daniel yelled from down the hall, "*Vamonós*! Time to go." Oscar shoved the towel in his beach bag alongside his bathing suit.

The car had been tight with the tall men and three girls in the back, but it had been better than driving around in the packed buses with unpredictable air conditioning.

When they arrived at the beach they went into the changing rooms to get ready for the water. Daniel had to show off his physique before anybody else and had taken off his shirt the instant they had arrived in the beach town.

They chose a spot to have lunch in a brown hut by the water. The location could not have been more perfect. They decided on a paella and had 40 minutes to kill before it was ready. Daniel ran all the way to the water, splashing the large waves against his body and making a lunge forward with stomach leading. Oscar waited at the edge, walking with all the females towards a spot where the cooler sand who soothe the burning on the bottom of their feet.

The towel came out of the bag and was laid out towards the south, facing the water.

Monica was simultaneously laying out her towel and jumped on it to relieve her feet. Oscar was looking at Daniel wrestling with the waves and felt Monica's fingers entwine his, while her free hand pointed toward the water. Oscar followed her steps, which increased from walking to running and within seconds they were wetting their skins with salty refreshment that burned their lips.

The Swedish girls lathered each other with lotion. They removed their tops, the underneath now the same shade as the lotion, white, very white, the color of the light in the sky. Their breasts were small, with matching size nipples and instead of making a sexual revolution, they appeared lacking and not matching the voluptuous dark-haired beauties that flanked them on both sides.

After all the lathering, they finished off with their backs and lay on their tummies for a while.

Oscar and Monica walked back, racing each other to get to the towels and stopped before they arrived to see that the towels were exactly the same. Oscar told her the whole story, hoping she'd not find the details creepy or strange.

"*No importa.* I think it is kind of sweet that you noticed the silly towel and then bought one to remind you of me. If we had never met again, all you would have had was the towel."

"Instead, I have all this!" Oscar picked up Monica and twirled her in a circle. She twisted her body to escape his arms, but he scooped her up, and they were back again in the water, kissing and laughing.

Monica floated softly in the water. The salt was so thick that it suspended her magically. Her skin sparkled, and small beads of water dotted her body, not mixing with the coconut tanning oil. She had no jewelry on, simply a bikini; two pieces of clothing separated Oscar and Monica from infinite possibilities.

On the drive back they took the scenic route, ascending into the Alpujarras Mountains, and visiting the famous *Suspiro del Moro*. Monica explained to Kim and Anna the story of Boabdil. Daniel started wailing and doing an impression of the young price and made the group burst out in laughter.

The next town they passed was Lanjarón. "What is this famous for?" Oscar asked.

"Lanjarón is a water bottling company. They sell it to all of Spain. The people who don't want to buy anything Catalán always say, 'If it sounds French, then don't buy it. Buy Lanjarón.'"

Oscar remembered seeing those bottles in the bar the night before.

They passed through rows of power windmills, dotting the landscape with new technology amid olive trees and grapevines. The girls were getting crushed as Daniel would accelerate through the curves and stop abruptly to point out some lambs or horses. They continued until a sign said, *Orgiva 10 kms*.

Daniel explained, "We are really close to Orgiva. There is the craziest festival here. The local townspeople hate it, but it has put Orgiva on the map. It happens every March close to the Equinox and is called the Dragon Festival. I have been twice, and I would totally recommend it if you are ever in this area during the spring."

Monica said, "I went this year and it was super fun. They say it doubled in size. It was pretty packed. After the festival we drove up to the Alpujarras Mountains and were freezing, with snow all around us."

Daniel said, "I swear Granada is the perfect city, with the beach half an hour away, the mountains to the east, great skiing and the best-looking guys."

Monica and the girls rolled their eyes but laughed regardless. Oscar patted Daniel on the back. "Thanks, tour guide, for the explanation."

Anna and Kim wiggled out of the back seat when they arrived in front of their hotel. "You should come visit us in Stockholm," Kim said between many goodbye kisses.

"Yes," the others agreed, even if they suspected they would never see them again.

XXI

The next morning, back at the house, Oscar and Daniel sat at the breakfast table.

Daniel laid out two plates with toasted bread. He poured olive oil, sprinkled salt and placed a piece of *jamón* on each slice.

"See how the *jamón* is sweating like us?" Daniel said pointing. "The only way to do that is to let it out of the fridge a while before you want to eat it. In the summer you don't have to wait as long, because it is so bloody hot!" he said, wiping his forehead with his shirt.

"I guess I shouldn't complain. My other option would be to live in England and the summers there are still rainy. I remember one summer there were only 5 days with sun. It is not that people stopped going out or anything, but I love the sun and could not imagine living in a place like that all year round," Daniel explained.

"That is where your dad is from, right? Does he still live there?" Oscar asked. The moment had come. Oscar had suppressed Alejandra's conversation in his mind long enough.

Daniel bit his bottom lip. "Yes, he does. He has pretty much since the divorce, so if we want to see him we have to go over there," he drank a full glass of water and then set it down slowly.

"Your mom talked to me about him. She told me this crazy story that my mom and him had met in England. Do you know about this?"

"Yes, of course. That is why we are here. I found those postcards two years ago and she told me the whole story. Oscar, I was afraid you would run away after my mom spoke to you."

"Why would I? I have nothing to be ashamed of. It has been a fun adventure to meet you, but you can't expect me to believe this whole story. Sure, they met, but that is not a big deal. Even if they had an affair, this guy, your dad, is not my dad. It is all a mix-up. Like the incident when we got off the train. Remember the craziness of being taken from jail to jail? I guess the criminal Oscar Santos is still somewhere on the loose," Oscar said.

"He may be, but all of this is no mix-up. I searched for you for years. I didn't just accidently run into you," Daniel explained.

Oscar interrupted, "Are you joking?"

"Sit down please." Daniel wiped his forehead.

"I am fine standing." Oscar adjusted his body, standing taller than before.

"I will start at the beginning," Daniel exhaled, "A few years ago, I had to renew my passport. As I was looking for my birth certificate in my mother's closet, I came upon a large green folder stuck behind two dusty leather purses. There were old letters and photographs inside and I turned the folder upside down to fit it back in the corner. Out came a thick bundle covered in black tissue paper. Inside were letters addressed to my father. The first few letters were romantic, and it was clear that he and a woman named Odette were keeping their affair a secret. Then she wrote a short letter to tell him she was pregnant. He received one last letter after the pregnancy news. She was clearly upset that Lawrence had ignored her correspondence about the baby."

"I think this is all a coincidence of names," Oscar shook his head.

"There are no coincidences here. The letters show the truth. Wait here," Daniel bounced out of his chair and left the kitchen.

Oscar thought of his other options. He could leave at this moment and never come back. He did not have to be part of this circus show of lies. On the other hand, he wanted to see the letters. This would give him some proof. He thought of his archeology professor who quoted David Hurst Thomas, 'It is not what you find, it's what you find out,' he would stay purely for the mystery of it. However, no proof could convince Oscar that this man, Lawrence, was his father.

Daniel returned with a dark green folder in his right hand and a large stack of papers in the other.

Oscar took his time, sorting the letters by date and then reading them chronologically. Unequivocally, the handwriting was his mother's. Oscar felt as if he were watching a movie unfold. Back and forth they spoke of how beautiful it had been to meet, how it was wrong, but that they must see each other again. There were dozens of letters. Then there was the letter about the pregnancy.

Dear Lawrence,

I don't know how to tell you this. I am pregnant. I have rewritten this letter and ripped it ten times. Words can't define how I feel. My tears are all over this paper and smearing what I write.
I ask nothing of you in terms of responsibility. I will keep this secret forever, but thought you would want to know.

Yours, Odette

Oscar read and reread the letter. The date on the envelope was October 2, 1972. He ran numbers in his head. He was 25. Nine months prior to his May 6, 1973 birthday would put his conception around August 1972.

Oscar pressed his lips tightly and leaned on the chair beside him. He felt light-headed and realized he needed air, so he took a deep breath and stuck his head out of the window. He couldn't look at Daniel. Instead he counted the number of clothes drying wires that hung up and down the atrium four floors above him. Across the way, the clothes were so tiny; they most likely belonged to a baby boy. The shirts were green and blue and had cars and dogs. Oscar remembered a photograph in his living room of his father and him. He was about four years old, was wearing a shirt with a Dalmation and red shorts. His father was picking him up about to throw him in the air. Oscar pulled on the clothesline outside the window. It squeaked, and Oscar took all the clothespins and aligned them close to him. Then he rearranged them and divided them by color and did the same with the second line.

Oscar could hear Daniel shifting in his chair. Oscar said, "I didn't expect the letter to say things so clearly. Perhaps there is a chance that she got pregnant when she returned."

He reached for a paper and pen on the counter and swiftly jotted down some numbers on a piece of paper.

Daniel spoke, "See, I am a leftie too, and so is my father. I am not saying that this proves anything, but look at us, we are not identical, but our body shape is the same. None of my brothers are as tall as me. Aren't you much taller than the rest of your family?"

"Yes, but that doesn't mean anything. Tall people could come from short families. Plus, how do you know what my family looks like?"

"Here, I don't want to scare you with all of this data, but remember that I told you I was a private investigator?" He handed Oscar a large stack of multi-colored papers. "It took me a long time to find you and to collect all of this information. I didn't want to approach you until I was sure that it was really you. So I made a plan to go to Lisbon. I couldn't figure out how I was going to speak to you and start a conversation, but I thought I would figure it out when I arrived."

"This is insane," Oscar said.

Daniel continued, "I arrived to the Lisbon train station at the crack of dawn. There were no beds left on the overnight train, so I ended up sleeping against the window for 15 minutes at a time throughout the night. I arrived to Lisbon so exhausted, and all I wanted was a coffee. As I was waiting in the café line, I saw you walking down towards the platforms. I thought I was losing my mind and delirious from no sleep, but something inside me told me that it was you. We have the same walk! I can't explain it. I followed you until you chose the last wagon and went a few paces behind you. You sat down and I passed right by you and went into the adjoining wagon. My heart was beating out of my body. I thought you would recognize me, or would notice that I was following you."

"I had no idea. I was in my head, thinking about the trip, where I wanted to go, and if I had forgotten anything. I can't believe you were following me!" Oscar said.

"If you found out you had a brother, wouldn't you go look for him?" Daniel asked.

"Daniel, I don't know what I would do. I am trying to process everything. This seems like a story you are making up, I feel dizzy," Oscar was leaning against the windowpane. Daniel pulled the chair by him and offered him a seat.

"Honestly, I didn't even know where we were going! I found a seat and chatted up the guy next to me and figured out the destination. I made up several plans to approach you and walked in to your wagon twice, but was so nervous I couldn't speak. When we arrived in Badajoz, I saw you put your backpack in the lockers, so I figured you had a long wait until your next connection. I went to the bathroom and looked for a change machine for the lockers. It was only a few minutes, I didn't think you would leave right away. I searched through the entire train station, but you were gone. I flipped out! How the hell was I going to find you now? One thing was going to your home city and creeping around until I found you, but now we were outside of your home base, and I had finally found you and lost you within hours. I didn't know what to do. Should I leave and roam around the city or wait for you there? I am a pretty impatient person, but I was determined that you needed to go back for your backpack, so I thought that was the only constant in this crazy equation."

"Were you really waiting all day? What was it, like five or six hours? Maybe less?"

"It seemed like forever. But I buckled down and thought, 'I have gotten this far, I am not losing him again.'"

"I thought you were so strange, yelling and causing a commotion at the train station." Oscar recalled the scene.

"I was desperate. I just started yelling at that moment and that is what came out. I guess I am a pretty decent actor, because you believed me. It was pure luck that there was an empty room at your hostel."

"What about that strange train trip? Did you veer us in the wrong direction purposely?" Oscar asked.

"Yes, I thought that anything that gave us more time would let me get to know you better," Daniel said.

"My goodness," Oscar said, exasperated.

"One thing I did not cause was the situation where we went to jail. That was random chance," said Daniel.

"I thought you may have set that up with your buddies, since you tend to hang out with criminals," Oscar said.

"I really don't, but honestly, if his sentence would have been heavier, we could have visited our father there."

"Don't call him that. He is your father, not mine," Oscar said with disgust. "Why the hell would Lawrence be in jail?"

136

Daniel quickly responded, "That is another long story!

"At first, my father was a business man. He worked for this British company that insured other bigger companies. It is a little confusing. Anyway, he made a pretty descent wage for Granada standards. The company started having some problems several years ago and my father was accused of these problems," Daniel said as he sat down.

Daniel grabbed the paper napkin in front of him and started folding and refolding it as he looked around the kitchen, mainly out the window but not towards Oscar's eyes.

"Okay, so then what?" Oscar was starting to feel claustrophobic in the kitchen.

Daniel continued, "The company was important enough that they insured the insurance company who managed the British Museum. It is still unclear exactly what role my father played, but let me tell you what happened."

"Yes, get to the point," Oscar said impatiently.

Daniel continued, "In March 1991, he went on a trip with three colleagues and they visited the Museum. The very next morning it was discovered that certain private papers from an old Dickens collection had been stolen.

"It ends up that my father was in the same room that day. According to what he told the police, he was cataloging the Bauzá Collection and never touched the Dickens section. The Bauzá had maps from the 1700's relating to Spanish America, Philippines, and some other stuff. Point is, he was never assigned to work on the

Dickens journals, but somehow they accused him and the other two men of stealing."

"What happened?" Oscar said, wondering how there could have been a mistake.

"Well it is kind of like our situation the other day getting off the train, except you had a really good barrister on your side," Daniel said trying to lighten up the topic.

"I don't think we would have been in that situation if you hadn't purposely put us on the wrong trains to Granada." Oscar's voice was full of anger.

"Could be," Daniel said apologetically and took a deep breath. "As I was saying, my father should have had a better defense. His other two work colleagues used the best barristers they could find. My father was so confident that it was just a big misunderstanding. He ended up being in jail for a while, until everything got cleared up and that is when things started falling apart in our family. My mother never believed he was innocent. She had often caught him in lies, and my younger sisters and I had witnessed them fighting. So, the girls and I sided with my mother. I was young at the time, barely in high school. My older brothers, Joel and Gabriel, were at the university and were not aware of the fights. They ended up siding with my father, and this created a huge division in our family. I have rarely spoken to my brothers since father went to jail. He killed our family unity." Daniel paused and then said, "That bastard."

Oscar did not like the sound of that word. It repeated in his head, over and over. His body and mind were raging.

In that moment, Alejandra walked through the door singing with a duster in hand.

"Pero, que pasa aquí?" she said startled.

"I was just saying goodbye to Daniel. Thank you, Alejandra for your hospitality. I... hope to see you again," Oscar left the kitchen and packed his belongings in a hurry down the hall.

Alejandra and Daniel argued in the kitchen. When Daniel saw that Oscar had left, he ran quickly to the living room window and screamed out his name. Oscar never turned around.

"I am going after him," Daniel scrambled to find his house keys and phone on the messy table.

"No Daniel, let him go." Alejandra put her hand on his shoulder.

XXII

The train station's chaos comforted Oscar. He did not want to be near Daniel or his messed up family any longer. He was free to go anywhere he liked. With plenty of money in this pocket, his only limit was his imagination. He studied the Departures timetable up above him. The white numbers and letters kept changing, and his brain started to spin with them. He heard the announcement, "Final call for Track Five, destination Málaga." It was his lucky number. He boarded without further thought.

He phoned Monica and explained that he and Daniel had gotten into a fight and he would let her know of his whereabouts once he was settled. Upon arrival, Oscar checked into a small hostel two blocks from the beach. His room was simple, everything white with a twin bed and a small desk and lamp. On his second night, he met a group of travelling *Lisboetas,* and they spent every night doing the same thing. The Pachá disco club was followed by breakfast at 5am. They would usually sleep until noon and repeat the day again. The days blurred with sun, sea and sangria.

He met many Spanish girls and even more foreigners. No matter the amount of beautiful women and temptations, Oscar kept thinking of Monica. After several phone calls and texts, he convinced her to meet him in Málaga. Tonight she was due to arrive.

Oscar picked her up at the train station, and they went to dinner at a small restaurant he had discovered a kilometer from the central beach.

"I'm starving!" she said as soon as she sat down.

"Calamares fritos y boquerones en vinagre por favor," Oscar's Spanish improved daily.

"Explain again why you left so abruptly. It didn't make sense to me," Monica said, sipping her cold white wine.

Oscar was taken aback for a second. No matter how many times he had tried erasing the conversations with Daniel from his mind, his sober moments betrayed him. He worked hard at obliterating the thoughts during the day, but they greeted him promptly every morning.

"Daniel and I didn't meet by coincidence. He followed me until he found me in Badajoz." Oscar looked at Monica, awaiting her surprise.

"No lo creo! Imposible! Why would he be following you?" Monica shook her head.

Oscar explained Daniel's reasons for finding him, the encounter in the train station, travelling together and their days in Granada. He explained Daniel's theory that they were half brothers and his own disbelief.

Monica listened with no interruptions. Oscar continued, "It still seems surreal to me. If it weren't for you sitting in front of me, I could blame this all on a dream. Or a nightmare," Oscar said, looking out at the sea. The waves were almost inexistent. He wished they were mightier like the Atlantic waves that crashed upon Portugal in a rage, white-capped and angry from travelling from the Americas afar.

"So, what are you going to do? I am sorry, I am still a little confused. Why would Daniel think you are brothers?

I know that your parents met, but how did he get that theory?" Monica asked with a concerned look.

"One of the letters that my mom wrote Lawrence said that she was pregnant and that he shouldn't feel he had any responsibility," Oscar said.

"Wow Oscar, I am not really sure what to say. Do you believe all of this?" Monica looked concerned.

"No, I don't. I acknowledge that it is my mother's handwriting, but I know in my heart that this man is not my father."

"What now? Are you still talking to Daniel? Does he know you are here?" Monica asked.

"No, he doesn't, and I don't plan to ever speak to him again. Any of this news, even if it is a lie, would destroy my family. My parents are happily married." Oscar listened to the words he had just said and wondered if he was the one telling a lie. He quickly smiled and shook his head free of those thoughts.

"What next? I promise I will be back to Granada to see you before I return to Lisbon, but first, why don't you come with me to Morocco. It is very close to here. Will you join me?" Oscar asked and finished his beer in one gulp.

"I would love to, but I have to head back and help my sister. She is having a really hard time managing the two *diablillos* on her own. The dad is not really around much."

"*Te entiendo*. It is fine, family is important. You are a good sister," Oscar held her hand and the word sister

142

echoed between his ears. During this whole time, he had not really thought of how this news would affect Elena. He silently prayed that she would never find out. His family was so important to him; he never wanted this to break their union. The betrayal he felt from his mother could not, would not, overshadow the family dynamic. He would take this news with him to the grave.

"I am so glad you came to visit. Are you ready to have some fun? These Portuguese are a little *loucos*. I think you will get along," Oscar held Monica's waist as they strolled along the boardwalk.

They joined the group and did what they had done every night. The repetition was comforting. The bartenders knew him by name, the songs were the same, and the heat enveloped them. Oscar's ears no longer felt the ringing; it was a constant hum and murmur.

The dance floor was not only filled with dancers but with bubbles. The floor was slippery and the crowd happily swayed with the beat pushing bubbles up in the air. Beautiful women of all colors danced slowly on the top of columns. Their outfits were white. They didn't even bother to follow the rhythm. If they danced too quickly, they would fall down into the crowd.

Oscar kissed Monica's full lips and they danced between the bubbles. Their bodies never separated until the morning sun and they ate their breakfast in a daze, consuming their bodily hunger on Oscar's twin bed. They moved quietly, as they could hear the guests in the next room talking.

Monica whispered, "I'm really happy to be here."

Oscar responded, "I am the lucky one. Thank you for travelling down. I missed you."

"Sure," she lightly punched him on the chest, "with so many beautiful dancers, I am sure I was always on your mind."

"You were. Look who is with me now. The most beautiful of all the women. Monica, *você é linda.*"

"*Si, si claro!* You are just using that Portuguese accent to make me like you more. You know what? Something has changed; you seem different than before. Not in a bad way, just not the same."

"I am a world traveller now!" Oscar smiled in the dark. "I guess maybe you are right, I don't feel the same." The sounds of other guests in the hostel could be heard: thumping feet, talking, and the clinking of glasses. "Come here!" he scooped Monica towards him.

"I can't get any closer," she said, giggling as her arm was stuck underneath Oscar's body. They made love again, this time less quietly, and they awoke naked with the full sun streaming on their faces.

After breakfast, they walked to the train station. "Are you sure you have to go?" Oscar caressed Monica's hair through his fingers.

"Yes, I promised my sister. But, don't be a stranger." She got on her tiptoes to give him a kiss.

"You probably won't even remember me when I go back to Granada. I am sure you have many suitors awaiting your return." Oscar smiled.

144

"Yes, tons! Especially when I walk around with two little devilish boys. That is a great way to pick up men!" Monica said.

"It worked for me." Oscar kissed her again, not wanting to let go.

"*Última llamada para Granada, línea dos,*" the loudspeakers announced.

"I have to go, I have already changed my ticket once, I don't think they will let me do it again," Monica said.

"I will see you soon, I promise," Oscar admired her at arm's distance and then kissed her while the bell was ringing. Her hand in the distance waved goodbye, and with every second it grew smaller. Oscar waved back.

XXIII

The weekend in Morocco did not end for Oscar when his Lisboeta friends headed back to Portugal. He thought, This is a new continent, I may never return again, and thus decided to explore more of Morocco. He headed south, visiting Rabat, Casablanca and finally ended up in Marrakesh. The food cost almost nothing, and the hostels were not busy. It was now September and hotter than his mother's temper. She was upset at him for not contacting home for several weeks. Oscar had not found the words, avoided the situation, and it had made his eventual phone call worse. Now things were being repaired; he wrote an email from the internet café, as phone communication was not accessible.

"I am in Marrakesh. Do not worry; everything is great. Mom, I am safe and will be returning home in a few weeks. I can't wait to give you the good news. The university emailed me and I got the assistant position in the Archeology Department. I start October 1st. Send love to Dad and Elena, Oscar."

Oscar was ready to go back to Lisbon, but not yet. He looked at the email on his screen and was finally ready to respond. Daniel had contacted him two weeks ago. It was clear he was saddened by Oscar's sudden departure.

Oscar surprised himself with his response.

Hola Daniel,

I write to you from Marrakesh, I never thought I would make it this far. I will be honest, meeting you is not what I expected from this trip, but ultimately it would have happened at some point. I see how persistent you are.

146

I have thought about it, A LOT. This may seem like an impossible request, but I want to meet Lawrence. I am not saying that I believe he is my father, I would simply want to meet him. I know he lives in England, but at some point you had told me that he visited your old house in Alicante. Not too far from Granada, perhaps 4 hours? I am so far away right now, that four hours seems a short time.
I don't know how you feel about this. I know your relationship with him is not perfect, but selfishly, I think that meeting him will give me some closure.

Write me with your thoughts, Oscar

Days passed and there were no emails from Daniel.

A week later, Oscar was in Tangiers. He had arrived to the port early in the morning.. There were no clouds in the sky and he could see the coast of Spain across the Straits of Gibraltar. He was surprised the boat ride would take an hour; it seemed so close.

He walked into the café and ordered fried eggs with cumin, pancakes with honey syrup and an iced coffee. This had become his favorite drink.

With several hours before his departure, he roamed around and spotted an internet shop. His hunch was correct, an email from Daniel was at the top of his screen:

Dear Oscar, I won't say that this has been an easy week for me but I am now feeling optimistic. You surprised me with your request to meet Lawrence. I should have expected it, but somehow it surprised me. I do understand now.
So, he said that he would be willing to meet and it so happens that he was already planning to visit our house in Alicante. Mom and him split the times, so they will never run into each other. He arrives on September 15th.
Email me and let me know if you are still up for it. I am not

working right now, so I am as free as ever.

Daniel

Oscar wrote back with a definite yes. He informed Daniel of his current location and made a plan to meet and head eastbound towards Alicante.

Oscar expected it to be uncomfortable after his sudden departure, but Daniel greeted him warmly.

"I wasn't sure if I would see you again," Daniel said, shaking his hand.

"I know. I needed some time to get away," Oscar said and reached forward to give Daniel a half hug. "I can't believe everything I have seen in the last weeks. I loved Morocco. Have you ever been there?" Oscar asked, while putting his backpack and small rug in the trunk of Daniel's car.

Daniel had never been to Morocco, so Oscar recounted everything he had seen and done. They spoke about Daniel's lack of employment and Oscar's new job.

"Dad, I mean, Lawrence, said I should move up to England, that there is a lot more work there. I don't know, it just gives me a bad vibe. I am not sure if I would want to leave Spain. It is sunny here, but, yeah, not many jobs. Honestly, I still don't know if I even trust what my father tells me. I have been waiting for him to fess up to stealing those documents. Maybe I should not be that hard on him. Perhaps we can't deny our DNA."

"What do you mean by that?" Oscar asked.

"Remember the whole story about the university? Me stealing the exams and all that? That tendency was not anything I was taught. I inherited it in my blood, in my veins. I am not a carrier of free will, only fulfilling my destiny of being a thief. You see, this was not the first time I had stolen. When I was little I would come home with all sorts of things. I remember being five years old and bringing a ring home for my mother that was at the antique store. She finally took me to the store to return it, hoping I would learn the lesson not to steal.

"I am no more at fault of being a thief, than you are of being a saint," Daniel exclaimed.

"I would hardly call myself a saint," Oscar said, "True, I have never stolen anything, but that doesn't make me a saint."

"Have you ever thought of killing someone?"

"No! Have you?" Oscar exclaimed.

"Sometimes, I wonder what it would feel like. To steal their last breath, but it is because I try to put myself in the mind of a killer, that is another reason I became a detective, to understand the motivations, to see the ability of the human to be closer to an animal than to his expected civilized self."

Oscar looked out the window and said, "Well, I am sure I am not a saint, neither are you as evil as you want to portray yourself. Let me tell you about the dream I had last night. I can't tell you how many dreams I have been having since I met you. I think I have been trying to sort out my life while I sleep, since I was partying so much when I was awake!"

"Do I kill someone in this dream?" Daniel took his eyes off the road to look at Oscar.

"No, you don't. This dream is set in Portugal. There I was in a large open field in the Algarve, actually high above a beach embankment that led to the ocean. The place was really beautiful in person, but in the dream everything was dark, the ocean was rough with crashing waves at the bottom of the cliff, and shark fins could be seen in the distance. Poor sharks have been labeled as evil animals; now nobody can take away their reputation. I was not by myself. You were there; you looked different. You were blond with light eyes, but I was sure it was you," Oscar explained.

"So you and I are standing at the edge of this cliff. It is so apparent to us that something bad is going to happen. The winds pick up, and we feel them pushing us over. You are much thinner too. I forgot to mention that. You fall over the edge first but catch yourself by gripping the rocks on the edge. I try to help you back up but feel the winds pushing me forward, towards you. All of a sudden I hear music in the background. It is this Portuguese singer called Camanes."

Daniel anxiously asked, "Ok great, the singer is in the background, what about me, do I die falling off the cliff and end up breaking my skull?"

Oscar continued, "Well, I guess I am not sure. I feel my body moving backward and I am far away from the edge so I can't see you anymore. I am pushed towards the music, the singing and it becomes so loud that I end up closing my eyes and covering my ears. When I open them, everything is quiet and I am no longer high up on the cliff. I am walking in the city, in Lisbon, and it is crowded and my phone rings and a voice I cannot recognize tells me to head towards the port. This is a part of town that is not that far from the center, but I rarely visit it since it is quite industrial and very busy and hard to get through.

"I walk over there and honestly am not sure what I am supposed to be doing there, looking for somebody or what is going on. I try phoning back the number that has called me and there is no answer, just endless ringing. My eyes are searching around, but with no direction. I don't have any glasses on and it is midday. The sun is now hurting my eyes. There are large ships moving in and out of the port, and at the far left are the cruise liners. I feel ridiculous just standing there, and start walking back to the city. In that moment, I receive a text: "Continue left to the cruise ship named *Blanca Mar.*" Realizing that I am being watched, I look about but there are so many people around and I figure that whoever is following me must be watching me from above, perhaps in one of the surrounding ships or buildings. Regardless, I continue on this wild goose chase. I near the cruise ships, and I see a small rowboat. It looks odd amongst the big ships and in it is a man. I think it's you."

Daniel said, "So, is it me? What am I doing on the rowboat? I thought I was shark bait at this point."

"I get closer to the rowboat, maybe even call your name, but your hair is in your face. Maybe you are sleeping or dead, again, I am not sure, but then somebody passes by me, bumps me hard enough where I am turned around, and when I look for the rowboat it is gone."

"Then what?" Daniel was getting more interested and wanted Oscar to explain it more quickly.

Oscar paused, trying to remember any forgotten details. "So, there I was back on track searching for the *Blanca Mar* and still walking towards the cruise ships. All of a sudden there is this loud sound coming from the ocean. Everyone around me stops and covers their ears as they search for the source of the sirens that indicate an emergency. I have never heard a louder sound in my life. I am surprised it doesn't wake me out of the dream. Groups of people in front of me are pointing towards the *25 de abril* bridge. I take one hand off of my ear to shade my eyes and see that the lights on top of the bridge are flashing. This goes on for five minutes that seem like an eternity as I am losing my hearing. Then nothing, silence and everyone starts to move around again.

"I think the cruise passengers have gotten really nervous because they are descending the stairs and heading toward me. I start to get scared. They are pushing past me, toward the mainland, trying to get off the large dock that connects then to steady ground. I am not sure what to do, so I wait and let them pass me. There are hundreds of them, mainly older people with white hair, but they are moving quickly. They must be scared because of the sirens, but nothing has occurred. I am getting impatient and as the crowd lessens I head closer to the first cruise ship. The name is something in Italian. I can't remember what it said. I check my phone to make sure that there are no new messages. My heart starts beating faster as I near the next ship and I recognize the first letter B. This is it. I look up and see that there are no passengers aboard. Suddenly, I see somebody start to descend the stairs. I am still standing at the bottom step and as the person gets closer I realize that it is you! You take each step very slowly, half laughing with a sinister smile. You still have that blonde hair, which looks almost like a wig. You are wearing a hat on top of it and a bright white shirt with a pin on the pocket."

"Am I by myself?" Daniel asked.

"Actually no! There is someone hidden at the top of the stairs and you glance backwards and signal with your head for them to stay hidden. The person crouching above has long dark hair. I don't remember thinking of it much during the dream, but it may have been Monica."

"Then what happens?" Daniel quickly looked at Oscar.

"Well, you get closer to me, and I think my eyes are playing tricks on me when I read the pin on your shirt." Oscar said, "It says, Capitán Oscar Santos."

"What?" Daniel said.

"Yeah, weird, right? Even stranger is that I don't mention anything. I feel threatened by you, but you instantly smile and say, 'I will take that," and grab a white leather suitcase from my hand. It has a bunch of peeling touristy stickers on it: Madeira Islands, a British flag and the pyramids. Then you compliment me on my shirt. I look down to see it has flower patterns on it; the type a tourist would buy at an airport store. When I look up, I see the police uniform hidden underneath your shirt and you are holding something shiny in your hands."

"What is it?" Daniel interrupted.

Oscar chuckled, "A pair of handcuffs."

XXIV

Granada was now far behind them. They had passed small *pueblos* and now found themselves amongst an arid scenery. Their destination was the area of Alicante. Located on the Costa Blanca, there were many beach towns that dotted the coast. The town where they would find Lawrence was called Torrevieja. Daniel described their many summers spent there among his siblings. Just like his parents' marriage, the town had been destroyed by greed, self-interest and lack of commitment to the preservation of its original habitat. The beach destination had been transformed from a quaint fishing town to a sprawling big city tourist trap. Daniel explained to Oscar how Spain's politicians had grown rich from receiving payoffs for illegal construction and how poor urban planning had destroyed the natural beauty that had made it attractive to begin with. This was repeated up along the coast.

Daniel assured him, "It is not as nice as it used to be, but it is still beautiful, and you must experience warm water. Your Atlantic Ocean is much too cold!"

Oscar said proudly, "The Atlantic Ocean is exciting, and we have great surfing. Lisbon really is a marvelous city. You must visit some time, your 15 minutes in the Lisbon train station don't count! "

"If you would have stayed put, I planned to visit more of Portugal, but you had to get on the train right after I arrived!" Daniel exclaimed.

"I guess that is how it was meant to go. You are always telling me how great Granada is, but did you know that Lisbon is the oldest city in Western Europe?" Oscar asked, waiting to see if Daniel would doubt him, as most did.

"Really! I had no idea. What about Rome or Athens? Aren't those much older?" Daniel asked.

"Actually Athens is not considered to geographically be in Western Europe. Politically, yes, but it is in Southern-Eastern Europe. Rome is in Western Europe, but Lisbon is still 400 years older."

"I had no idea, so is Athens older than Lisbon?" Daniel was curious.

"Yes, it is, but our claim is to be the oldest city in Western Europe. Athens is the oldest in the East," he said.

Daniel said, "I wonder why nobody really talks about it. Maybe it is because then we would have to give importance to Portugal, and Spain is wider and fatter and just acts like the harassing big brother."

"Exactly, like you!" Oscar said, the words coming out before he realized their significance.

Thinking of Daniel as a brother was not painful. It was comforting, in a strange way. Oscar had always wondered what it would be like to have a brother. How would his life have been different?

Oscar looked at Daniel fidgeting. His hands held the stick shift and then played around with the air-vents. Their hands were very similar, with slender, long fingers that would fit the piano keys perfectly. Oscar's hands were roughed up from working many years at his father's bakery. Healed burn marks were faded, but deep cuts still showed the scars. His pinky leaned toward the left. Although his parents had sent him directly to the emergency room, the doctors had told them that the heavy

155

machine that had fallen on his hand would always cause a slight angle in his smallest finger. In turn, Daniel's hands were smooth and tanned and showed many hours of holding books and pens, of white-collar labor.

Oscar did not say anything for a while. He pretended to read his magazine but kept staring at Daniel's hands. Were these external limbs the best indicator of our soul? Did his show a life less advantaged than Daniel's? Or was he more prepared for the journey or life? Maybe eyes were not the windows as had always been written. It was true, eyes could be shaded with sunglasses, women would paint them and stretch the skin around them, and one could try to lie with their eyes. Show them smiling, or cry crocodile tears. But hands, how did one hide their true state? Gloves could cover them, but once removed, the true evidence of life was there, like the rings of a tree.

XXV

"So this is really your first time outside of Portugal in 25 years? When I was researching you, I showed you always at the same address since birth. Why did you decide to leave Lisbon when I arrived?" Daniel asked.

"I had no idea you were looking for me! I had always wanted to travel and see the world. My Uncle Nuno passed away suddenly and left me a good amount of money. I was not expecting it. I thought I should travel this summer, before I found a job. It all worked out, since I begin on October 1st. Wow, that is almost in 2 weeks!" Oscar said, realizing it was not that far away.

"You sure are a planner. Trying to outline your life step by step, huh?" Daniel said, making it obvious that he didn't prescribe to this way of life.

"No, well, I guess I don't consider myself such a planner. My trip has been anything but linear, a zigzag through the Iberian peninsula, ending in a hop over to Africa," Oscar was proud that he had seen so much; he felt older, more experienced.

The two-way narrow road ended and Daniel turned on a big roundabout that led them to a larger highway. He drove quickly and passed ten cars before arriving to the tollbooth.

"*Los últimos serán los primeros,*" Daniel said, raising his fisted hand.

"We have a saying just like that! I can't remember how it goes. Do you know what *Devagar se vai ao longe* means?"

"No, what?" Daniel said, trying to translate in his head.

"It means, 'He who treads softly goes far.' It must be my favorite saying," Oscar said, looking forward as their landscape started changing.

"Let me think, I guess I must say, '*Santa Rita, Santa Rita, lo que se da, no se quita*.' I like it when they rhyme and I like my poetry to rhyme too. Supposedly, it is no longer in fashion to have your poetry rhyme, but as with all things, this too will change." Daniel changed subjects like a politician.

"What does that saying mean?" Oscar said, having been distracted by the poetry comment.

"It means that if you give something, you can no longer ask for it back," Daniel translated.

Oscar wondered if given the choice, he would have preferred to be blind to the affair between his mother and Lawrence. He felt torn. Was it better to know the truth or live in a comfortable bubble? He looked out the window and felt connected to the strange view. The rolling green hills were gone. He could no longer see the olive trees, the open dry land, or the birds flying overhead. There was clarity with only the bare earth. They were surrounded by tall, square-like formations, made of dirt, and with no vegetation in sight. The setting looked like a background for a western movie. It was barren and empty, and it made him think of a Clint Eastwood movie he had seen at home with Elena. She had grown so bored with it and asked him to turn it off. But he was enjoying it and liked the slowness of the scenes and that feeling of the land to be discovered. She was finally annoyed by the movie and his interest in it and left the room. He watched the end by himself: a few more deaths, and then horses appeared, taking them away, towards the sun. That was the only western he had ever seen. Was it four years ago? He made a mental note to try to watch another one soon.

Oscar took a drink of his water because even though the air conditioning was on full power, he was still sweating. It was impossible to escape the heat. "We will have to stop soon. We are out of water," he pointed towards their empty water bottles.

XXVI

"Ok Dani, I am starving. We need to stop soon. It is past two p.m. We can take a break to eat and still arrive in the afternoon for a swim." Oscar said, beginning to feel light-headed.

Daniel was hungry too. "That is fine. Let's pull over up ahead. I think that looks like a restaurant?" Daniel pointed.

But when they neared the 'restaurant', it was just walls of wood resting on each other. From the remains, it was unclear what this building had been in a past life.

They drove around a bit more and saw a sign, *Casa del Rojo,* with a black hand-painted arrow pointing down an obscured road.

"That means Red House, but do you think that is a place to eat?" Oscar asked. Everything looked vacant. They had not passed a single car since they had left the main highway.

Daniel said, "Let's at least try it. If it is not a place to eat, at least they can tell us where the closest one is."

"Sounds good to me," Oscar said as he shifted around in his seat ready to stretch his cramped legs.

Open sky stretched between the far mountains and the road, which had turned into a bumpy, dirt trail. After driving another 500 meters, Oscar questioned whether that had been an old sign.

"Let's drive a little longer and if we see nothing, turn around." Daniel said, and before he could finish his sentence a row of buildings appeared on the left side. The roofs were an orange and dark yellow alternating design. Memories of white stucco walls were covered with dust, and the windowpanes were encrusted with stones. There were solar panels on top and birds' nests lay between them.

They parked alongside two cars and three white motorini. The entrance door was covered by a curtain of braided beads, a thin protection against the insects outside. When they passed the threshold, the beads moved like waves and made the same sound.

The room was empty except for the sound of music playing on an ancient radio. They went toward the radio in the back corner but realized that it was turned off and that the music was coming from outside.

When they passed through the beaded curtains, they were caught by surprise. A thin man was playing the guitar, and there was an older couple in front of him watching him play. The young men must have looked parched because within minutes they were sitting alongside the man and drinking cold water. The lady, who had introduced herself as Sara, brought them salted almonds and dates. The sugar, salt and water seemed just what their bodies needed, and they expressed their gratitude several times.

"*Mucho gusto,*" Daniel said, accepting the hand of the older man.

"*Me llamo Gustavo, pero todos me llaman El Rojo.*" The man scratched his narrow chin that was covered by reddish orange hair. His beard looked like it had grown for a long time but was still sparse. The top of his head was impressive, filled with red curls placed on top so neatly as if he had curled each one and secured them with hairspray.

Daniel explained to Oscar that the old man's real name was Gustavo but everybody called him 'Red'. Oscar shook his hand, and el Rojo introduced him to Jaime, the guitar player.

Once everyone sat down, Jaime resumed playing. His fingers glided over the strings with ease. Daniel knew quite well the strength needed to play this instrument. He told Oscar that he had tried in his youth to play but had blamed his thin fingers for the lack of ability. Oscar described the same feeling. They agreed that the piano was the instrument most coveted by their identical hands.

They ate *cocido*, a dish made of garbanzos, pork and a variety of vegetables. Sara explained that it was usually eaten in the winter, but she had made it two days ago to last all week.

"We don't go to the big city very often, so I get creative with the food." Sara smiled and gave them a second helping and filled up their glasses with red wine.

Beyond the patio where they were sitting was a garden with rows of vegetables and fruits, most already harvested alongside bright orange and lemon trees. Umbrella pine trees shaded the stone path. It could have been straight but the stones were placed in a continuous S form, the reason for which Oscar did not inquire about. Connected to these trees were hammocks and el Rojo encouraged them all to go use them.

"*Sentaros en ellas, son comodísimas,*" el Rojo insisted.

162

Jaime's guitar music hypnotized Oscar and Daniel as they rocked side to side to side.

El Rojo and Sara swayed on a wooden swing covered with handmade pillows. Only Jaime was still, sitting on a leather stool. The patio was shady, cheating the sun of its power. A faint breeze reached in over the walls.

El Rojo started singing to Jaime's music. He had a rough, cigaretty voice. He sang three songs and everyone applauded when he finished.

Sara's accent was difficult for Oscar to comprehend and Daniel translated.

"Did you just say, 'a fortune teller?'" Oscar asked.

Daniel replied, "Yes, Sara just told me that people come from far to visit her and was wondering if we came to have our fortune read?"

"Hmm…" Oscar paused, unsure how he felt about this topic. He had never had his cards read. His mother did not believe in any of that and called it hocus-pocus. "What do you think?"

"I am not sure. I have never done that before," Daniel replied.

"Me neither. Tell her *sí*. Even if it is all made up, it may make for a good story," Oscar said.

Sara placed a colorful shawl over the round wooden table. She shuffled the card deck and asked Oscar to cut it; then she arranged the cards slowly in rows.

163

"We see the Death card, but don't be afraid. It does not necessarily mean death of the body, but rather a transition, a big change that is occurring. There is rebirth within, when something dies." She explained in Spanish and Daniel translated.

"Well, that is obvious, this big bomb of news you dropped on me. I almost wanted to kill you, maybe you are the dead body she is talking about," Oscar said and winked at Daniel.

Sara pointed to a card with a soldier, "Here is the Knight of Swords. His card has appeared upside down. Take caution. This Knight tends to be hasty and impulsive. He will make decisions without thinking of the consequences. Is there a decision you must make shortly?"

Oscar and Daniel looked at each other. Oscar spoke first, "I don't think so, we have had to make decisions lately, but I don't think there is a big one in the future." Oscar wasn't convinced of the words he had uttered. He had decided that meeting Lawrence would help him come to terms with the news of his affair with his mother. He was also convinced that he would not mention any of this to his parents. Would his mind be changed when he arrived in Lisbon?

El Rojo offered them sweets and an after-dinner drink. It reminded Oscar of the yellow liquor he drank on his first afternoon in Badajoz. A novice traveller he was no longer.

Oscar and Daniel nestled in the hammocks, and found sleep before she had invited them in.

XXVII

Perhaps it was a few minutes or an hour, but when they awoke there was no sound from the guitar, complete and utter silence.

"We should get going," Daniel said.

"Yes," Oscar responded, rubbing his eyes and stretching himself out of the hammock.

"*Que tal dormisteis?*" Sara said with a gentle motherly smile.

"*Muy bien, gracias,*" Daniel said and apologized for overstaying their welcome. Sara made him feel at ease and explained that Jaime was gone and had bid them farewell and el Rojo was napping in the building next door which was also their house.

Daniel asked for the bill, and Sara said that there was no charge. They insisted on paying, but she ignored their requests, saying that the food and wine were 'on the house.' Sara waved them goodbye as they left, and they wound around until they found the highway heading east.

"Was that really strange?" Oscar asked.

"*Pues sí.* I am just glad you are along on this ride, or nobody would believe what we just saw. I bet if we tried finding this place again, we would lose our way in dusty paths. The whole thing was surreal," he said, looking forward and not at Oscar.

"I know exactly what you mean," Oscar said smiling.

They finished the last part of their drive and were exhilarated when the coastline appeared.

They passed lagoons and mountains of salt in low ponds that Daniel described as a major source of income for this area. Luck was with them, and they found a parking spot in front of the entrance to Daniel's family apartment.

The layout was very simple, with three rooms, two of them filled with bunk beds, and one bathroom. The best part was a terrace that opened up to the Mediterranean Sea. It was beautiful beyond words. Oscar took pictures and then turned the camera on himself and Daniel and they took a photo together.

"I don't know why I have not been taking more photographs," Oscar said. "I think I will start today. That way I will better remember the trip."

"Is there a call center nearby?" Oscar asked after they unpacked and opened up all the apartment windows.

"Yes, it is just down the street. I'll show you where it is, and then you can meet me at the beach," Daniel explained.

The call center had five doors inside and a small desk area with four computers. Oscar wondered why it was called an internet café, when there was never any coffee. He chose door number 5. Daniel sat at one of the computer stations.

Oscar's mother answered on the third ring. "Oscar, *meu filho*! I am so happy to hear from you. Where are you now?" her voice a mix of happiness and worry.

166

"I am in Torrevieja. It is directly east of Lisbon, but on the Mediterranean Sea. How are father and Elena?" Oscar asked.

Odette described their busy work life. She said Elena was out with friends and that the house was not the same without Oscar. They were all awaiting his return.

"Hold on, your father is here," Odette said and passed the phone to Edmundo.

"Oscar, how are you? Your mother is driving me crazy. She showed me your emails, and I told her you were fine. I am glad you are travelling so much. That is what your Uncle Nuno would have wanted. I am so glad you are coming home soon. I bought front-row soccer tickets to see the Sporting Lisbon play Real Madrid. I couldn't wait to tell you the news. You know I am not good at keeping secrets." Oscar agreed.

"Gracias Papa," Oscar's heart hurt a little thinking of all the secrets so recently discovered, but it brought a smile to his face. "*Eu sinto sua falta*," Oscar could not remember the last time he had told his father that he missed him.

"*Eu também*," Edmundo said with surprise in his voice. "You aren't going to start rooting for the Spanish teams now, are you, son?" Edmundo chuckled.

"No, I am always on your side," Oscar said with clarity of heart and mind.

Oscar walked south towards the sun. He passed the marina and watched the boats in the distance; the sky was blue and clear, with no memory of clouds. He found the beach that Daniel had marked on the map. It was known as *La Playa de los Locos*. The name was appropriate. How he had ended up in this small fisherman's town was a crazy occurrence. Oscar removed his shirt and sandals and dove into the Mediterranean Sea. Ripples of water cut the stillness and tickled the feet of the ducks near the rocks.

Oscar was at the eastern most point of the Iberian Peninsula. He had never expected to travel this far. Pride filled his veins, he felt like an explorer. He had found the answers to questions he had never asked. He no longer had to look in the mirror and wonder why he didn't look like his family. Edmundo was his father, blood or not.

Daniel joined him at the beach, informing him that Lawrence's flight arrived at 10 a.m. the following day. "He is going to meet us over there at *Montebianco*," he pointed to the white and blue café, "I hope he recognizes me. It's been over four years. He might end up liking you better."

"Thank you," Oscar said to Daniel.

"For what?" Daniel asked.

"I didn't think that I would ever thank you for finding me, but you have helped clarify many things in my life. I am proud to call you my brother."

"*Gracias hermano*. You can't disappear on me again. I am an unemployed private investigator with a lot of time on my hands!" Daniel hugged Oscar, and they ended up wrestling on the beach until they collapsed, panting on the shore. A wave splashed over them, washing away the sand and their doubts.

ACKNOWLEDGEMENTS

This novel is not an island. It surfaced from the seas through the efforts of many people. Here is my list, in no special order:

To Nina and Martha, who were there at the beginning. To Susan Odgers, Daniel and all of the Michigan Writers, and TC Authors. Thanks for your writerly encouragement. To my editor John Pahl, thanks for your dedication, hard work and moments of stories and laughter. To Colleen Zanotti, this beautiful cover design is the cherry on top. Thank you for years of working together, and mostly for your friendship. To Jacque Burke, your back cover photograph will keep me young forever. I can't thank you enough—you are my motivator extraordinaire.

To Dulce, Toni, Katy, Shawna, Lindsay, Pippa, Jala, Laura, Sarah, Hjarsti, Oksana, Shannon, Angie, Nicole, and all my TC friends. Thank you for making the snow seem like sand.

To the Stantons: Doug, who picked up the phone when he saw a number from Beulah as if it had been from (212). Your kindness has not gone unappreciated.

Nancy, Michael, Bones, Drie, Bob, Julie, & Casey. An awesome family of in-laws & outlaws. You make me feel so loved. Thanks for all the great times together and for officially making me International Call.

To the Niemans in Miami, the Mullens and Calls in the Midwest and to the Gonzalez in Spain. Your love and support transcends the miles between us. A special mention to the Guercios: the first to buy my novel. To my cousin Jorge: the first Spaniard. To my readers in Europe: Mil Gracias. Mille Grazie. UCSB friends Nicole, Nikki, Erin, Cecilia, Stacey, Jen, Wendy, Karen, Scott, Nick & Joy: 21 Forever!

To Paola, Giordi, and Isabella Nicole Camerini in Italy. You have made my life better every day since the moment I walked up to the terrazzino on Via dell'Argilla. To Margarita: you know why.

Jaime, Elena, Ulysses y Leo: Although the distance separates us, I take you in my heart everywhere I go. Fratello, a life without you as my almost twin sibling would have been meaningless.

Mami y Papi: Sin vosotros no estaría aquí. Sois unos padres estupendos. Las palabras no pueden expresar cuanto os quiero y aprecio la vida tan bonita que nos habéis dado a Jaime y a mi.

To Sofia: If I could have painted a picture of my dream daughter, it would not be as wonderful as you. Te quiero Coco.

To Winston: I feel so lucky to have you. You are the cutest and coziest boy a Mama would ever want. Thanks for keeping me in the Club.

To Warren: I should dedicate a page of this just for you. Our story is one for the centuries. You are not my best friend, you are my media naranja, mas guapo y valiente que el Principe Azul. Thank you for being strong and bright in my roughest hours at sea through this book and all my endeavors. *Tu eres mi faro en la oscuridad.*